HC

A FOOL AND HIS MONEY

1924, Cornwall. When a man is found dead from gunshot wounds on Hunter's Path, a picturesque spot in Falmouth, it's up to Inspector Bartlett and Constable Boase to find out whodunit – and, more importantly, why. The dead man, Clicker the Clown, was the main attraction at Martin's Circus – and with his reputation as a kindly and well-respected old soul, who would want to kill him? As Bartlett and Boase investigate, they discover old enmities and a close-knit community which doesn't want to give up its secrets ... even if that means the gallows for some.

A FOOL AND HIS MONEY

A FOOL AND HIS MONEY

by

Marina Pascoe

Magna Large Print Books
Long Preston, North Yorkshire,
BD23 4ND, England.

British Library Cataloguing in Publication Data.

Pascoe, Marina
    A fool and his money.

    A catalogue record of this book is
    available from the British Library

    ISBN   978-0-7505-4230-2

First published in Great Britain in 2016 by Accent Press Ltd.

Published in Large Print 2016 by arrangement with
Accent Press Ltd.

Magna Large Print is an imprint of Library Magna Books Ltd.

Printed and bound in Great Britain by
T.J. (International) Ltd., Cornwall, PL28 8RW

Dedicated to the Memory of

PC Andy Hocking

Respected member of the
Falmouth Police Force

Friend to many

Chapter One

'Marley was dead: to begin with. There is no doubt whatever about that... Old Marley was as dead as a doornail.'

'No, Daddy, NO! I don't like dead people.'

Peter Trevarthen looked at his father, tears welling in his eyes.

'Peter, you know the teacher said you have to read this because you're going to be in the play. You can't be in it if you haven't read it.'

'But dead people frighten me.'

'Well, yes, but they can't hurt you – only the living can do that.'

Charles Trevarthen looked at his son and closed the book. He didn't suppose that he would have enjoyed this when he was nine either.

'Maybe we'll try again tomorrow – there's really nothing to be afraid of. Now, why don't you go off to sleep?'

'I can't sleep – I'll dream about dead people. Daddy, will you leave the door open?'

'All right – just this once. Goodnight, Peter.'

'Night, Daddy. Are we going to the circus tomorrow?'

'Yes, if you're a good boy, of course. I'm quite looking forward to it myself.'

Leaving the bedroom door ajar, Charles Trevarthen crossed the landing and went downstairs.

'He won't read that book, Violet. As soon as he

11

knew it was about dead people, he refused to have anything to do with it. I really don't know what's wrong with him.'

'Charles, you know he's been strange about death ever since your father died. He can't help it.'

'Yes, dear, I know – but that was two years ago. He should be over it by now. May isn't behaving like that.'

'But May is eleven.'

'Could you talk to him again, dear – perhaps tomorrow?'

'Yes, Charles, of course. Why don't we leave it until after the circus has been – maybe that'll cheer him up a bit?'

'Very well.'

At half past seven the next morning, Constable Archie Boase crossed the Moor and headed for the Falmouth police station. He paused outside the library to look at a poster advertising Jeremiah White's circus. He might enjoy that; he hadn't been to the circus since before the war – now it was 1924. Yes, the last trip to the circus must have been in about 1910. As Boase walked on towards his destination, he wondered if his fiancée, Irene, would like to go with him ... he'd ask her tonight.

Inspector George Bartlett was already in their shared office when Boase arrived. Having vowed for some time to retire and spend more time at home with his wife, Bartlett *still* couldn't give up. The strange thing was, he didn't know why. He had mused, no, agonised over the decision for some time now and yet couldn't bring himself to stop. Superintendent Greet had been dropping hints – but then, he would. The two men were never in a month of Sundays going to get along together. Well, maybe it was *because* Greet was pushing that Bartlett was standing firm.

Archie Boase tossed his hat towards the hat stand in the corner. It promptly fell to the floor.

'Boase, you have been trying that every day for the past twelve months – you can't do it.'

'Well, I will eventually. I just need more practice.'

Bartlett looked at the younger man over the top of his reading spectacles and grunted.

'Cuppa, sir?'

'I wouldn't say no. I've been here half an hour and Penhaligon hasn't even offered. Have you seen him this morning, Boase?'

Boase had passed Constable Ernest Penhaligon in the lobby on his way in. He had been deep in conversation with Father Patrick O'Malley, the new Catholic priest at St Mary's church. Boase poked his head around the door and saw Penhaligon heading towards the office with a tea tray.

'Good man.'

Boase held the door open wide and patted the constable on the shoulder.

Bartlett cleared a pile of papers on his desk with one movement of his hand and gestured to the constable to lay the tray there.

'Thanks, Penhaligon. What was that about with the priest?'

'He's in a right state, sir. Apparently someone broke into the church in Killigrew last night and stole the Blessed Sacrament.'

'What? You mean the Communion?'

'Yes, that's what he said. Apparently Canon Egan is distraught – couldn't even come in here himself to report it.'

'Well, did anyone see or hear anything?'

'Father O'Malley says not, sir. The lock was broken on the side door and that's obviously where they got in. Canon Egan is in a very bad way – and he's such an old man. He's just sitting in the church apparently and won't even speak.'

'I hope he's all right.' Bartlett poured milk into the cups.

'Father O'Malley says Mrs Donnelly is with him – the cleaner, I believe.'

'Boase – shall we stroll up there when we've had our tea? We want to nip this in the bud – can't have people going around stealing from churches ... whatever next!'

'But this is a particularly terrible crime, sir.'

'Is it? No one's dead.'

'Well, no. But all the same.'

Boase took the cup of tea handed to him by Bartlett and Penhaligon left them alone.

Bartlett and Boase took the short walk up Killigrew and to St Mary's Catholic Church. They walked around to the side door; the wooden frame had been broken.

'Looks like someone's had a jemmy to this, Boase.'

Bartlett pushed open the door and, removing his hat, walked into the church. Boase followed. In the front pew sat a small, old man, his hands covering his face. The two men approached him.

'Canon Egan?'

The man looked up. His face was tear-stained.

'Yes ... yes, I am Egan. You are...?'

Bartlett introduced himself and Boase.

'I understand you've had a break in – we thought we'd come up to have a look. Has anything like this ever happened before?'

Canon Egan mopped his head with a handkerchief.

'I have never in my life seen anything like this, sir. I have been a priest in this county for almost fifty years and I have never heard of such a terrible deed.'

The rattle of a cup in its saucer caused the three men to turn. The cleaner, Mrs Donnelly, stood with a tray.

'Now, Father, I've made you a lovely cup of tea. Come on now, you've had a nasty shock. Drink this and you'll feel better in no time.'

'I really don't want any more tea, Mrs Donnelly. Nothing will make me feel better.'

Bartlett took the cup from the woman and, sitting in the pew next to Canon Egan, offered the old man the tea.

'I think Mrs Donnelly's right, you know. Drink the tea and, if you don't mind, I'll just ask you some questions. Is that all right?'

'Yes, thank you. I'll drink it.'

Bartlett opened a small notebook and licked the tip of a pencil.

Boase, meanwhile, had wandered off to the back of the church and was looking at the Stations of the Cross. This all brought back memories – his first Communion, his confirmation. It was all so important back then ... and now ... and now, well, after being in France during the war he had changed his mind about all this. Well, he thought he had. *How could God allow all those things to happen? Why didn't he stop it? How could he allow such horror and human suffering?* Boase turned these questions over as he examined the broken door. He returned to the small group in the front pew.

'Excuse me, Father, was the ciborium taken too?'

'Oh, yes, dear me ... yes, it was. I suppose that was probably what they really wanted. You see, they broke into the tabernacle to get it, so they knew what they were looking for and where to find it.'

Bartlett leaned forward towards the old man.

'Did you not hear anything at all?'

'No, but you see these walls are very thick and my hearing isn't good.'

'When did you last see everything as it should be?'

'Well, I was in here last night at about half past ten, I suppose, just checking everything as I always do.'

The small group turned as the side door of the church was pushed open and a tall, thin man swiftly crossed to them. He placed both his hands on Canon Egan's shoulders.

'Oh, my word, what can I say? I've just heard the terrible news.'

'And you are?'

Bartlett had stood up as the man crossed to them.

'I'm so sorry, I'm Martin McCarthy – I'm the

organist here.'

Mr McCarthy held out his hand to Bartlett and then to Boase who introduced themselves.

Bartlett turned to the organist.

'Can you shed any light on what might have happened here last night, Mr McCarthy? As you can imagine, Canon Egan is very shaken up.'

'Oh, I can imagine he is.'

At this, McCarthy patted the old priest's arm.

'I really have no idea about who could have done such a terrible thing, really I haven't. We have such a lovely congregation here – oh, but of course...'

At this he broke off and looked up to the altar.

'What, sir?'

Bartlett looked at the man, enquiringly.

'Well, nothing really, I was just thinking – you know the circus is here, I suppose?

Boase nodded.

'Yes, we've heard. What has that to do with any-thing?'

'Well, some of those sorts were here yesterday for the morning mass. Some of them looked a bit rough, I thought.'

Bartlett felt not a little irritated at this observ-ation.

'Well, that doesn't make them criminals, sir.'

'No, of course not, I'm so sorry. No, it doesn't. It's just that there were several people here that we don't normally see. That's all.'

Canon Egan interrupted the conversation as he stood up.

'Would you forgive me, gentlemen? I do have things to attend to. Is that all you wanted?'

'Of course.'

Bartlett took the teacup from Canon Egan and handed it to Mrs Donnelly.

'We'll obviously do anything we can – leave it to us.'

'I hope you can retrieve everything, Inspector. Please do your very best.'

'Rest assured, we'll do everything possible.'

Bartlett and Boase left the church and walked back down Killigrew.

'You a religious man, Boase?'

'Catholic, sir.'

'Well ... I never knew that – you still go to church?'

'No, no I don't – feel quite bad about it, actually.'

'How so?'

'Well, my parents brought me up in the faith and I feel I've turned my back on it all – since the war, really.'

'That's perfectly understandable, my boy – I know just what you mean.'

'Doesn't make me feel good though. I used to be an altar boy.'

Bartlett chuckled but tried to keep a straight face as he stopped to light his pipe.

'You? An altar boy? I suppose you have got a sort of angelic little face.'

Bartlett's shoulders heaved up and down as his laughter became more uncontrollable.

'All right, sir, joke over. Now, what shall we do about this break-in? Poor Canon Egan, I feel sorry for him. Mrs Donnelly grabbed me just as we left and whispered to me that he has a bad heart.'

'Well, something like this won't do him much good then, will it? He must be nearly ninety if he's a day. We'll set about it this morning – you get someone to talk to the neighbours first, see if anyone saw or heard anything.'

'Right, sir, will do.'

As the two men reached Berkeley Vale, Boase paused at yet another advert for the circus.

'Do you think Irene would fancy this, sir?'

'Why don't you ask her? I couldn't say, other than the last time we took her she was about eight; she cried so much Mrs Bartlett had to keep taking her outside.'

'Why was she crying?'

'She got upset about the animals – said they shouldn't be made to do tricks and suchlike. She said they should be in the jungle like the ones in her book.'

Boase smiled. That was just like his Irene; so sensitive and caring. Now he was worried she would say no. He'd ask anyway; if she didn't want to then they could always do something else.

Betty, Joan and Anne Warner passed around a bright red lipstick. Betty marked a thick stripe across the back of her hand.

'This is lovely, Joan. Where did you get it?'

'There's a little shop in the main street – near the church on the corner. They've got ever such a lot of nice things in there ... think it's called Robertson's.'

'Well, this is just perfect – can we borrow yours

19

tonight? I haven't got time to go there now.'

'Course you can. I didn't buy you one each 'cos I didn't know whether you'd like it.'

'That's all right, Joan. Look, Anne – what do you think?'

Anne, the youngest of the three sisters, took the lipstick and looked at it. She handed it back to Betty.

'Yes, it's very nice. I'll get one too.'

Betty put her hand on Anne's arm.

'You all right, kid?'

'Yes. Of course. Just a little nervous about tonight, that's all.'

The three Warner sisters had formed a juggling act when they were teenagers and had held shows in their back garden. When their parents died in an accident, the girls had used their skills to earn enough to support themselves. Then the circus came to their home town, Liverpool, and they were offered a place as an all-girl juggling act.

This suited Betty and Joan very well, but for Anne, who was now only seventeen, life was difficult and she missed her old friends back in Liverpool. She hated travelling around the country and didn't see the same adventure in the career that her sisters seemed to find. In short, she was a homebody. But then, as her sisters regularly pointed out, where *was* home? They had no home and no parents – so, for now, they told Anne to make the best of the situation.

Anne rose from her chair.

'I think I'll go and see Clicker. I've got a cake for him. See you later.'

The girl left and made her way to the small

caravan occupied by Clicker the Clown. She knocked on the door and waited. The door was soon opened and there stood the old man who had been the leading clown at this circus for over forty-five years.

'Anne. How lovely to see you, my dear. Come on in – what's that you've got there?'

'I've brought you a cake, Clicker – I know you love a jam sponge.'

'You know me too well, young lady. I've just put the kettle on, so we'll cut your lovely jam sponge and have a cup of tea. Sit down.'

Ann pushed aside some clothes and sat in the small armchair while Clicker fetched the tea and a knife for the cake.

'You all ready for tonight, Anne?'

'Well ... yes, I suppose so.'

'Now, you don't sound very sure about that.'

'You know I don't want this for the rest of my life, Clicker. It's fine for Betty and Joan, I think they rather like this life but, no, it's not for me. Oh! I'm so unhappy.'

'There, there, Anne dear. Here, have this tea and we'll cut some cake. Here you are now.'

'You know, Clicker, apart from you, there's no one else I even get on with in this beastly circus. It's all so hateful.'

'Well, I suppose I'm used to this life, I've been doing it for so many years – and I can't tell you how many youngsters have told me all about their lives, in this very caravan. Some of them have stayed, some of them have gone on to other things. Yes, I've even seen half a dozen of them born here – right into this very circus. For some of us, it's a way of life.'

'Well, it's not for me. As soon as I have enough money, I'm leaving this horrid place.'

'I really wish I could help you, Anne. Really I do. But, well, with Margaret in the sanatorium in Switzerland ... well, let's say it's costing me rather a lot of money. I can't really spare enough to visit her. But Molly says she's getting better. Maybe one day soon Margaret will return to England.'

'Is Molly still asking you for money?'

'Well, yes – and I feel I have to pay it. Anything to get Margaret well again.'

Anne was only the person in the circus, other than Molly, to know about Clicker's past. When he was a young man he'd had a romance with Margaret Field. Billed as the most daring high wire act in the world, she and Clicker had spent almost a year together. They had made plans to give up this life for something a little more conventional but then Margaret, discovering she was expecting Clicker's child, disappeared. He had received one letter from her the following year telling him of their daughter, Molly. He had kept the letter all those years, heartbroken that he would never again see the love of his life or his daughter.

His world was turned upside down again when, seven years ago, Molly arrived looking for her father. When she found him she seemed to be happy and, with her husband, joined the same circus as trick horse riders. Clicker felt he had at least found some happiness with his daughter close by – and she looked so much like her mother.

Things went well for a few months, then the demands for money started. Molly had told Clicker that her mother was very ill in Switzerland and that she could no longer keep up the payments for her mother's care. Clicker hadn't hesitated; this was the least he could do for Margaret. And so, most of his money earnings went to Switzerland while the old man lived a frugal existence, pretending to be happy and funny just to earn enough to pay the bills.

Anne looked at her watch.

'Oh my – I didn't realise how late it's getting. Time just flies by with you, Clicker. You always make me feel better. I must go and get ready. Thank you for the tea – and good luck for tonight.'

Clicker grabbed Anne's arm.

'Anne, don't stay here if it's making you unhappy. I'm so sorry I can't help you with money at the moment. If I could do it, I would, but I'm sure something will turn up for you soon.'

'I know you want to help but please don't worry. I'm sure you're right. I've already got almost ten pounds saved up – that's a start isn't it?'

'Yes, of course it is. Mind you keep it safe too.'

''Bye, Clicker.'

The old man closed the caravan door and drew the curtains across the tiny windows. It was time to get ready.

Peter Trevarthen held his mother's hand as they walked from their house on Greenbank and made their way to the recreation ground and to the circus. As May walked with her father, she looked

23

up at him.

'Daddy, are lions dangerous?'

'Well, yes, I suppose they are – if they escape.'

'Peter says lions can eat you.'

'Well, May dear, these lions will all be in the circus ring and nowhere near us – so you don't need to worry. What are you most looking forward to, Peter?'

'I think I shall like the clown best. I've got a book all about clowns. Do you remember, Daddy – Auntie Jane gave it to me when I was five, for my birthday?'

'Yes, as a matter of fact, I do remember.'

The family reached the entrance to the circus. Violet Trevarthen put her hands to her ears.

'It's very noisy, Charles.'

'Oh, no it's not, dear. Come on, you'll enjoy it when it starts.'

Chapter Two

The Big Top fell silent. The lights were dimmed. Nothing was happening. Everyone waited.

'CLICK. CLICK.'

A beam of light pooled in the centre of the circus ring and there stood a solitary clown. As he walked to the edge of the ring, his shoes could clearly be heard. 'CLICK. CLICK.'

Peter laughed loudly.

'Oh, Daddy – it's Clicker ... the clown on the poster. He's *so* funny.'

The boy's father smiled and looked at Violet. He winked, pleased that Peter was happy – at least for now.

Two more clowns joined Clicker, one of them driving a small car which promptly ran the other two over. Now even May was laughing – May who had said clowns were 'childish and not in the least bit funny'. As the evening wore on, more and more acts came out to entertain including the juggling sisters, the trick ponies, dogs, lions, elephants. By the end of the show, most children there were exhausted.

'Come along, you two – it's very late.'

Violet Trevarthen gathered up the children's coats and the family made for the exit. Peter ran on ahead, taming lions with a stick he had pulled from a hedge.

'May, I'm going to be a lion tamer when I grow up.'

'No you're not – that would be stupid.'

'Why?'

'Because it would.'

'Why?'

'Mummy, tell Peter to stop saying "why".'

'I think you're both very tired – you're usually in bed by now. Did you enjoy yourselves, dears?'

Both children expressed their delight at having spent the evening at the circus and both begged to go again next time. By the time they reached the house, Peter was asleep in his father's arms.

George Bartlett poured himself a cup of tea and lit his pipe.

'Cuppa, Boase?'

'Just had one, sir, thanks.'

Archibald Boase sat behind his desk and drew out a paper bag from his desk drawer. He carefully unwrapped it to reveal the contents, a large saffron bun.

'Want a piece of bun with that, sir?'

Bartlett looked over the top of his glasses at the younger man.

'No thanks, Boase – wouldn't want to take food from a starving man. My word, no – you might waste away to nothing!'

'All right, sir, no need to be sarcastic – I didn't have much breakfast this morning ... and I only had time for one cup of tea before I left.'

'Well, I just offered you another. Here you are, pass your cup.'

Bartlett walked over to Boase's desk with the teapot and filled the cup.

'I think we'll ask Penhaligon for some more, I'm rather thirsty myself this morning. Now, talk to me about the theft at the church.'

Boase took a small notebook from his pocket.

'Well, sir, I was thinking about this Mr McCarthy – you know, the organist.'

'Go on.'

'What he said about the circus ... do you think there's anything in that?'

'I don't know, but I suppose we shouldn't overlook it. When I was growing up in London we often had the circus coming to town – no one trusted them. I always thought they were a nice bunch of people on the whole, didn't seem to cause much trouble, although...'

'Although what, sir?'

'Well. People did say the crime rate went up when they were in town – just petty thievery really, nothing, what you might call dangerous.'

'Well, thievery is what we're looking at here, sir, and in the absence of anything else, I think the circus might be a good place to start our enquiries. After all, they'll be gone again soon and then it'll be too late. I thought I'd take a couple of men up there this morning – see if we can find out anything.'

'Right you are – I think I'll come with you.'

Within the hour, Bartlett and Boase were at the recreation ground and, together with Constables Coad and Eddy, were talking to some of the circus troupe. Boase went inside the Big Top where the trapeze artists were practising. He watched in amazement, almost afraid to look up at their antics on the high wire. He walked over to the group and spoke to a young woman.

'Excuse me, miss. My name is Constable Boase, from the police station. I was wondering if you could help me, please?'

The girl called out to the other members of the group who stopped what they were doing and came over. The girl, speaking in Italian, introduced Boase.

'My name is Allegra. This is my sister, Rosa, my brother, Angelo, and my father, Giovanni Marziani. If you want to speak to my father, I'm afraid I will have to interpret – he doesn't speak any English ... well, only a very little.'

Giovanni shook Boase's hand and said, 'Very little, very little.'

Boase told the family his business and about the break-in at the church. When Allegra explained to the father, he made the sign of the cross across his chest and spoke hurriedly.

'My father says he is shocked that someone could do this. We attend church as often as we can if we are not working. This is a terrible crime, constable.'

'Yes, it is, miss. And none of you can offer any help? You haven't heard anyone around the circus talking about it?'

'No, I'm so sorry – nothing.'

'I'm sorry to have troubled you all – thank you for your help.'

Boase walked towards the entrance to the tent and turned for one more look as the trapeze artists carried on rehearsing. As he left the tent, he saw Bartlett walking in his direction.

'Any luck, Boase?'

'No, sir, afraid not.'

'Have you made an account of who's here?'

'Yes, I spoke to the ringmaster, Chester Martin – he seems to be in overall charge. He says everyone here is well-behaved, never seem to cause any trouble – well, not *outside* the circus.'

'What does that mean?'

'He said that there are often altercations amongst the people who work here – you know the sort of thing, squabbles about the acts or money, but these things are always resolved.'

'So, who's here? I've just been speaking to the lion tamers – Pearl and Arthur Wayland. They're a strange pair … they were actually talking to me with three enormous lions roaring right next to me. I could barely hear a word.'

Boase laughed.

'Well, aside from them, there's, let me see ... there's the trapeze artists I've just been talking to – the Marzianis; they're very good, sir. Irene will love their act. Then, well, then there's the fire eaters, they're called Howard and Gregory Smith, father and son those two.'

'Have all these people been spoken to, Boase?'

'Yes, looks like it, sir. Where was I? Right, three sisters, surname Warner, nice girls. Also, erm ... here we are, yes – there's a high wire act, they're the Beauchênes ... French, I suppose they are. And there's a married couple called Edward and Molly James.'

'What do they do?'

'They do tricks on ponies or something I think, sir. Nearly at the end, wait a minute ... oh, how could I forget the clowns – the lead clown is called Clicker...'

'Real name?'

'It doesn't say here, sir.'

'You'd better have a word with those two constables.'

'What? Coad and Eddy?'

'Yes – looks like *they're* a right pair of clowns too. Their note-taking is dire. Did they add anything when you spoke to them?'

'No luck, they say, sir. I've sent them back now. Two other clowns called Billy Jones and Brendan Hoyle. Just one more character – ooh, we don't want to cross him.'

'Cross who?'

'Gwynfor Evans.'

'Why – what's the matter with him?'

'Well, he's Hercules – you know, sir, the strongman. You should see the size of him – about seven feet six, I'd say.'

'Really?'

'Yes, but the hilarious thing is, sir, he's got this little squeaky voice – really girly.'

Bartlett started to laugh at the thought of Hercules the Strongman having a girly voice. He pointed to the exit.

'Come on, Boase. We may as well join the two clowns back at the station – this burglary had nothing to do with the circus. We're wasting our time here.'

Clicker sat on the step of his little caravan and drank a small bottle of beer. He smiled as he watched Billy Jones trying to master the unicycle. As the younger clown fell to the ground for the seventh or eighth time, he turned to see Clicker laughing at him.

'I'll learn to do this if it kills me – and you can stop laughing. I've nearly got the hang of it.'

'How long have you had that bicycle, Billy?'

'About a year. I just need a bit better balance, that's all. I will get it in the act soon.'

'I'll be dead before that happens – I'm not getting any younger, you know.'

Billy fell once more from the bicycle and, picking up the source of his frustration and embarrassment, headed for his own caravan.

Clicker shook open the *Falmouth Packet* and quickly flicked through the pages. He liked Falmouth well enough. Yes, this might be the sort of place he would retire. But, wait ... no, Clicker would never retire. His family was right here in the circus. Everything he wanted was here. Well, almost everything. As he cast his mind back many years and thought of his beloved Margaret, a tear came to his eye and he hastily wiped it away, just in time to see Molly coming towards him. He stood up from the step.

'Hello, Molly. You all right?'

'Yes thanks. Better than Mum.'

'Oh no. How is she, Molly dear?'

'I had a letter from the clinic. Her doctor says she's up and down, you know. Sent me another bill too.'

Clicker sat back down on the step.

'How much is it, Molly?'

She pulled a sheet of paper from her coat and handed it to the old man. He drew some reading spectacles from his pocket and looked at the bill.

'This is such a lot, Molly dear.'

'I know – but I can't pay it. You want her to get better, don't you?'

'Oh, of course I do. But I also want to go to see her. I can't afford to travel to Switzerland when all this is costing so much.'

'Look, Dad. You and Mum had a thing going years ago – it didn't work out and that's not my fault. Why should I have to pay for your mistakes?'

'Don't be like that, Molly, please. I've tried to help you ever since you came here to the circus, you know that. But I haven't got pots of money.'

'Don't blame me for your shortcomings.'

'I would have given anything to be able to stay

with your mother – but she just left. I didn't even get a chance to say goodbye – or to even see you. I would have loved nothing more than to be a proper little family with you. I loved your mother so much.'

Molly snatched the bill from Clicker's hand and marched off. The old man turned, went inside his caravan, and locked the door.

'What time are you and Irene off to the circus tonight, Boase?'

'Well, I thought I'd call for her about six, if that's all right, sir?'

'Yes, that should be fine. Come in for a cuppa afterwards if you like – you should be out by about nine ... unless you have other plans, that is?'

'No, I don't think so, sir.'

Boase blushed and didn't know why. He and Irene Bartlett were engaged now – and he needed to stop blushing when anyone spoke of his lovely fiancée; no, that wasn't befitting a soon-to-be married man, rather a silly schoolboy.

'Any more news on the church business, my boy?'

'No, nothing at all. They've taken the precaution of extra locks on all of the doors – but that's literally closing the stable door after the horse has bolted.'

'Well, we'd better keep an eye on it. Come on, let's go before Greet finds us something else to do – we've been here quite long enough today.'

Boase didn't argue and the two men took their coats down from the stand and left for home.

At five minutes to six Archie Boase was knocking at the Bartletts' front door. He waited and heard Topper, the Airedale Terrier, barking from the other side. The door was opened and there stood Caroline Bartlett.

'Hello, Archie – how lovely to see you again. Come on in.'

Boase entered the hall and went forward into the parlour, negotiating Topper as he went. The dog picked up a red rubber ball and dropped it at Boase's feet.

'I can't really play with you in here, Topper boy – we might break something.'

Topper lay down and, resting his head on his paws, let out long sigh.

'Oh, I'm sorry, Topper. Have I upset you? I'm sorry. Here, have a little pat.'

Boase knelt on the floor next to Topper and patted the dog's head. Caroline smiled.

'You're very silly with that dog, Archie. Anyway, how are you?'

'I'm very well, thanks, Mrs Bartlett.'

'Archie! How long have you known me – it's Caroline to you.'

'Oh, yes. Sorry – I keep forgetting.'

Boase still didn't feel comfortable calling his prospective mother-in-law by her Christian name – any more than he could call his boss 'George'.

'Sit down for a minute, Archie. Irene will be here presently; she just went up to change her shoes.'

As Boase sat and waited, Bartlett came in from the kitchen.

'Evening, my boy. Everything all right?'

'Yes thanks. You?'

Bartlett signalled to a bottle of his beloved Leonard's London Beer on the sideboard and grinned.

'Oh, I'm more than all right – got time for one of these, Boase?'

Boase looked at the mantel clock which was just striking six.

'No, thanks, better not; we don't want to be late.'

At that, Irene came into the room. Boase stood up and looked at her.

'Evening, Archie – do I look OK?'

'Oh, yes, Irene. You look lovely.'

'Well, you're not so bad yourself. Shall we go?'

'Yes, come on then.'

Irene kissed her mother and father and then she and Boase went out into the hall. Caroline called after them. 'See you both later – have a lovely time.'

The front door was shut and the house was quiet. Topper, who had been to the door to see them off, came back into the parlour and lay down on the rug.

'I think I'll have my beer now, Princess. Can I get anything for you?'

'No thanks, George. I'll make myself some tea in a minute. They make such a lovely couple, don't you think, George? *George?*'

Bartlett was patting Topper on the head and concentrating on his pipe.'

'George!'

'Sorry, Princess, what was that you said?'

'Oh never mind. You're hopeless.'

'I'm sorry. You said something about them being a lovely couple?'

'So you *did* hear me.'

Bartlett chuckled and winked at his wife.

'Yes, they're a lovely couple. Any more idea when the wedding is going to be?'

'They haven't said. They don't even know where they'll be living yet. I suppose they could come here until they find somewhere of their own.'

'Now, Princess ... stop there. I love Irene more than my own life but I'm drawing the line there. We had to live with your mother, sneaking around like two schoolchildren for the first two years we were married ... don't get me wrong, I loved your mother but it wouldn't have been my first choice to live in her house. No. I'm putting my foot down. They'll have to find somewhere soon or delay the wedding – it won't hurt them to wait. We're getting old together – on our own! It's time I had you all to myself. They'll have to sort themselves out.'

Caroline didn't argue. She knew how Bartlett felt on the matter; this wasn't the first time they'd discussed it. She respected his thoughts and felt he was probably right.

Boase and Irene took the short walk from Penmere Hill to the recreation ground and joined the long queue for the circus. Irene slipped her arm through his and he patted her hand.

'Looking forward to it?'

'Yes, very much, Archie – I hope they won't be cruel to the animals. Do you think they look after them properly?'

'I'm sure they do – don't worry.'

As Boase spoke, he was watching two figures standing in the shadows. There was a young woman speaking intently to someone he could barely see. She was holding a newspaper up and the pair were looking at it. Suddenly she leaned forward to embrace the other person. Boase leaned further forward to try to see what was happening. Irene saw what he was doing.

'Archie – you must be the nosiest person I've ever met. Apart from Dad, that is. What *are* you looking at?'

'Oh, nothing.'

Boase continued to watch as the woman walked away and the other person came forward towards the queue.

'Look, Irene. That's Clicker – you know, the old clown I was telling you about. He looks a bit fed up ... do you think he's all right?'

'I thought clowns were supposed to be fed up – isn't that part of their act?'

'Well, maybe.'

Boase pushed Irene further forward in the queue and kissed her head. He didn't want to ruin her evening. *That was a strange business, all the same.*

The young couple were enjoying the circus immensely. Irene loved the juggling sisters. She whispered to Boase, 'I'd love to do something like that. Can you see me in a band of jugglers, Archie?'

'Um ... no, Irene – I don't really think I can.'

Irene poked him playfully and giggled. Suddenly the Big Top fell into darkness. A car horn was heard.

'PARP. PARP.'

'Oh, Archie – it's the clowns. Look, here they come.'

The crowd cheered and clapped as two clowns entered the ring, one in a funny little car, the other on foot – on very big feet. Suddenly the crowd fell silent. All at once they began to chant.

'We want Clicker! We want Clicker! CLICK-ER! CLICK-ER!'

The chanting was now accompanied by the stamping of feet as the crowd became louder.

As the people waited, a large spotlight lit up the ring and there stood the ringmaster.

'Ladies and gentlemen, boys and girls, can I have your attention please.'

They all listened and waited.

'I'm afraid Clicker can't be with us tonight. He's a very old clown and is feeling rather unwell this evening.'

At that, the crowd booed loudly and several objects were thrown in the direction of the ringmaster.

'Boo! BOOOO!'

'Ladies and gentlemen, boys and girls, please.'

As the ringmaster tried to gain some control over the situation, the people fell suddenly quiet and then burst into uncontrollable laughter. They had spotted the two clowns playing leapfrog, very badly, and one had got his enormous shoe trapped inside the coat pocket of the other. The ringmaster, seeing his opportunity for escape, fled to the back of the ring and was gone.

Irene looked up at Boase.

'What do you think happened to Clicker? You

37

thought there was something wrong.'

'I don't know – maybe he just wasn't well enough to perform. Hope he's OK.'

The pair settled down along with the rest of the crowd to enjoy the remaining entertainment.

Back at the Bartlett house, Boase sat down in an armchair and drank a cup of tea.

'You should have seen them, sir, it was hilarious – they were even throwing things at the ringmaster.'

'Well, I really don't know – what a carry on.'

Bartlett was puffing on his pipe.

'Why were they so angry?'

'Well, Dad, I suppose because Clicker didn't turn up – they say he's the star of the show.'

Irene went out into the kitchen. 'Anyone want more tea?'

'Not for me dear, I'm going up to bed – I feel quite tired.'

Caroline rose from her chair and, patting Topper on the head, went to the door.

'You all right, Princess?'

'Yes, I'm fine, George, dear. Goodnight. Goodbye, Archie – we'll see you again soon, I hope?'

'Yes, I hope so, Mrs Bartlett – I mean, Caroline. Goodnight. I should be going home too. Thanks, Irene – that was such good fun.'

Irene was leaning against the kitchen door.

'Yes, it was – I do hope the animals are all right. What do you think, Dad?'

'I'm sure they are, Irene – you don't know what to worry about next. I'm sure they're well looked after. Those lions I saw yesterday looked in pretty

38

good health, roaring right next to my head.'

'But don't you worry that they're supposed to be in the jungle?'

'Well, yes, sometimes – but then, when would people like us ever see them – except in zoos?'

'Well, that's another thing, though, isn't it?'

'Irene – don't start all that. It's getting late – I think I'm off to bed too. Goodnight both. Don't be long, Irene.'

Bartlett left the room and Boase and Irene kissed, happy to be alone again.

'I really have to go, Irene. I can't stay here all night.'

'I wish you could, Archie.'

'Oh, yes – so do I. Come on now, let go.'

He prised himself from her embrace and made his way out.

Irene walked to the front door and waved as Boase left through the garden gate.

Chapter Three

George Bartlett hung his coat on the peg in his office and lit his pipe. As he drew his chair to his desk, he called out loudly.

'Penhaligon ... Penhaligon!'

The door burst open and Constable Penhaligon stood there.

'You all right, Inspector Bartlett, sir?'

'Of course I'm all right – just wondering what I have to do to get a cup of tea around here?'

39

'Oh right, sorry, sir – I thought there was something wrong.'

'Well, there is – I'm thirsty. How's your mother coming along, Penhaligon?'

'She's very well, thank you, sir. Yes, thanks for asking – she's much better than she was. My sister Dorothy is staying on for a bit to look after her until she's completely well again.'

'That's excellent news, really it is – your mother is a lovely woman. Be sure to give her my best, won't you? Now, what about that tea?'

'Very good sir, it's on the way.'

Penhaligon closed the door and left Bartlett alone. The inspector puffed on his pipe and wondered what the latest on the church theft was – it had all gone very quiet. As he mulled it over, the door opened again. This time, it was Boase.

'Morning, sir.'

'Good morning, Boase. How are you?'

'I'm just fine, sir, but I've just had a strange story relayed to me.'

'Go on. I'm listening – Penhaligon's just making some tea. Tell me your "strange story".'

'Well, one of the circus troupe I met the other day came running after me down Killigrew.'

'Bit odd, that? Who was it?'

'Well, it was Billy Jones – one of the clowns.'

'What did he want?'

'He was just standing outside the recreation ground when he saw me passing on the other side of the road. He said that he was worried about Clicker – you know, the lead clown. He said he hadn't seen him since yesterday afternoon.'

'Is that a problem?'

40

'Well, he says Clicker is really reliable – he's been with the circus for years, man and boy. He says it's not like him to go missing. In fact, I saw him myself, last evening – when I was queuing up with Irene. He was talking to a woman and then he didn't turn up for the performance. That's what I was telling you about – the crowd went mad because he wasn't there – he's practically the star of the show.'

'Is this man worried about Clicker?'

'He seemed to be *very* worried.'

'Well, I don't think we can do anything yet – it might seem a bit premature. What do *you* think?'

'He's quite an old man, sir. Maybe we *should* be concerned. And it's out of character.'

'You think we should be looking for him?'

'Well, not a manhunt as such – but maybe we should be keeping our eyes open, asking a few questions.'

'You win, Boase. Let everyone know what's happened and to be on the lookout – but I think it's too early to start panicking.'

'Right you are, sir, I'll let them know.'

'Anything more on this church business?'

'Not a thing, no.'

Suddenly, hearing a scraping sound, Boase looked towards the door. He walked over and opened it to find Penhaligon's shoulder against it and the constable bearing a large tray. Boase held the door open wide enough to accommodate both man and tray.

'Thank you, sir. I've brought some goodies for you both.'

Penhaligon laid the tray down on Bartlett's

desk and the three men stared at it. There was a teapot, two cups and saucers and a large plate upon which were two sausage rolls, two large slices of fruit cake and two cherry buns. Penhaligon grinned at Bartlett and Boase.

'These are from Superintendent Greet. He said he thought we'd all appreciate a little treat.'

Boase stared at the constable.

'Let me see if I've got this exactly right ... Greet said he'd like to give us a little treat. *Superintendent Bertram Greet from upstairs?*'

'Yes, sir.'

Boase looked at Bartlett who shrugged his shoulders.

'Don't look at me – I'm as perplexed as you are. Just tuck in. Quickly, before he changes his mind. Thank you, Penhaligon.'

The pair finished all the food and drank the tea.

'I've never known you to eat this early, sir.'

'Well, shame to waste it – he's up to something though, you mark my words. Anyway, we need to get on, can't sit here all day. I've got some papers for you to go through, including an update for Greet on the church business. I need to have a word with those constables about their note-taking, too – I think I'll get that out of the way this morning.'

'Righto, sir.'

Boase removed a large pile of papers from Bartlett's desk and began to work on them immediately. Bartlett went to find the constables who were on duty in a bid to improve their note-taking and, he hoped, their handwriting.

42

As the desk sergeant looked at the clock above the bench in the outer office and saw it was half past eleven, a small boy burst through the main door of the police station and grabbed the sergeant's tunic sleeve.

'Oy, young man, I'll thank you to get yer 'ands off – I've just put this on clean this mornin' – what d'you want anyway, tearing in 'ere like there's bin a murder or something?'

'But there 'as, there 'as – 'onest there 'as, mister.'

'It's "Sergeant" to you, you little blighter – an' what d'you mean – there's bin a murder?'

The desk sergeant looked down at the boy who appeared to be about eleven or twelve years old, wearing a fisherman's smock, thick drill trousers and a peaked cap. His feet were bare.

''Ere ... aren't you one of them Barnicoat boys – you're Billy Barnicoat's lad.'

'Yeah – an' there's still bin a murder. Wot you goin' to do about it, mister?'

'I'll give you "Mister". Sit down over there on that bench and behave yerself.'

The boy sat down and the sergeant walked over and sat next to him with a notebook and pencil.

'So ... who's bin murdered I should like to know – and where?'

'There's a dead man. I've seen 'im. There's all blood comin' from 'is 'ead – loads an' loads of blood. I've seen 'im – 'e's up 'Unter's Path.'

'Well, 'ow do I know I can believe you?'

''Cos I'm telling the truth – really I am.'

The boy became less excited as the sergeant continued to doubt him and as the novelty of his apparent find wore off.

'So, can you show one of my constables where this body is? Could you take him there now?'

'Yes ... course I can.'

'You'd better not be telling me fibs young man – do you know you could get into serious trouble telling fibs to a policeman?'

The boy nodded.

The sergeant went to fetch Coad and sent him off with the boy in search of his find.

Boase stood up and stretched. He hated sitting at a desk shuffling paper. He'd rather be out talking to people, getting on with real police work. Still, this was all a part of his job. If he didn't spend so much time thinking about his lovely Irene then he might get on a bit quicker. He pulled open the top drawer of his desk and drew out a brown paper bag. He opened it to reveal a thick ham sandwich and laid it on the desk in front of him. As he considered whether he wanted the whole sandwich or just a half at this point, the door opened and Penhaligon stood there with a cup of tea.

'You read my mind, Penhaligon, well done.'

The constable placed the cup on the desk.

'Inspector Bartlett said he'll be in shortly – 'e's just finishing up 'is lecture.'

'His lecture?'

'Yes – 'e's bin goin' mad with everyone ... says we don't know 'ow to take notes.'

'Well, I can't disagree with him on that one.'

Penhaligon sighed and left the room. Within a couple of minutes, Bartlett returned.

'These young men, Boase, they think they know it all. Got an answer for everything. Well, I don't think we'll get so much trouble from now on – I've just told them straight. How's all that coming along?'

'All done, sir – thank goodness. I detest paper-work, I really do.'

As Boase picked up his sandwich, the door burst open and the desk sergeant came in, red in the face with Penhaligon standing behind him. He addressed Bartlett.

'I'm so sorry, sir, Coad has just been up to Hunter's Path with that Barnicoat boy who was in here this morning. There's a body up there, sir.'

'A body – well, who is it?'

'We don't know, sir. Coad stayed there and got word to us.'

'Come on, Boase – Hunter's Path, you say?'

'Yes, sir.'

Bartlett and Boase ran to the door of the station and got into one of two police cars that were waiting at the front.

After a short drive the police car drew to a halt underneath Pendennis Castle and Bartlett and Boase walked quickly to Hunter's Path and to-wards the precise location they had been given. Coad was waiting for them.

'What's going on here, Coad?'

Coad stood to one side to reveal the body of a man lying on the ground.

'He's been shot through the head, sir.'

Bartlett knelt down by the body.

'No trace of a weapon by the body so definitely

not suicide. We need to identify this poor chap as soon as possible. Boase?'

The younger man stepped closer to the body.

'Oh no! I know who this is, sir.'

'Who is it?'

Boase stepped back and looked at Bartlett.

'It's Clicker, sir.'

'Clicker? The clown? You sure about that?'

'Yes, sir, I am. I saw him only last night when Irene and I went to the circus.'

'I thought you said he didn't turn up?'

'That's right – but I spotted him while we were queuing. Irene saw him too. I never said anything because it didn't seem important. I just thought he was unwell – being so old and all that.'

'So, why on earth would he be here, shot through the head? Did he seem all right when you saw him?'

'I'm not really sure, sir. He looked a bit fed up – I said as much to Irene.'

'What was he doing when you saw him?'

'He was standing behind one of the caravans talking to a young woman. They were looking at a newspaper then she put her arms around him and they went off in different directions.'

'Right, well, we'll talk about that more later. Make arrangements to get this place examined and to sort out this poor old man.'

Having returned to the station, Bartlett and Boase sat in their shared office. Bartlett lit his pipe.

'So, where do we start with this, Boase? Any ideas?'

'Yes, sir. Plenty. I think we need to start with

those people at the circus – we need to get up there straight away.'

'I agree – that's a good starting point. Get some men together will you?'

As Bartlett and Boase walked up Killigrew and made their way to the recreation ground, Boase pulled a small pork pie from his pocket.

'You can't be hungry again, Boase. After all that food this morning?'

'Well, I just noticed this in my pocket this morning, sir – I think it's on the turn, so I thought I should eat it today.'

'You're going to end up poisoning yourself. Anyway, never mind that – who was this woman you saw speaking to the clown?'

'I don't actually know. I didn't get a proper look at her. I could tell she was young but I only really saw her from the back. I noticed she had long, dark hair. She was wearing a pale blue cardigan and navy trousers.'

'Well, that's something. Do you think she's a member of the troupe?'

'Difficult to say, sir. I've brought along a list of all the people we interviewed before so I think we should concentrate on the women first, maybe ... see if we can find her.'

'That sounds like a good idea, Boase.'

The two men, followed by three constables, had now reached the recreation ground. Bartlett gave the three men his instructions and then turned to Boase.

'Right. Who are the women on your list?'

Boase flicked through a small notebook.

'Well, we've got, let me see, there's the trapeze artists – two of them are women. That's Rosa and Allegra Marziani – we could start with them. Then there's one of the lion tamers, Pearl Wayland. Also one of the high wire act … erm, wait … yes, here she is, Adele Beauchêne. Plus three sisters who juggle – Betty, Joan, and Anne Warner. Then just one other, I think – Molly James, the trick pony rider or whatever they're called.'

'Right. Come on, let's make a start. What's the chief's name?'

'It's Chester Martin. Look – over there.'

Boase indicated a caravan with the ringmaster's name painted on the side and the two men crossed the field towards it. Bartlett knocked. The door opened and a rather shabby little man stood there. He was wearing brown trousers with braces hanging loosely by his sides and a grubby, greyish vest. Boase was astonished that this could be the dapper man he had seen in charge of the big top the evening before.

'Yes?'

'Good afternoon, Mr Martin. We've met before. I'm Inspector Bartlett and this is Constable Boase.'

'Yes. I remember you. What do you want?'

'Can we come inside please, Mr Martin?'

The man opened the door and Bartlett and Boase went inside the caravan. The smell of stale food pervaded the small compartment which was being used as a sitting room. Bartlett moved a pile of papers from a bench and sat down. Boase remained standing.

'I'm sorry to say we have come here with some

48

bad news, sir. Please sit.'

'What is it? What's happened?'

'I'm afraid it's about a member of your troupe – Clicker. I'm very sorry to tell you that he was found dead this morning.'

'Dead? Clicker? No. No – you must be mistaken. I only saw him yesterday.'

'I've been told that he didn't perform last night?'

Chester Martin looked at Bartlett.

'Yes. That's right. I wasn't told. He didn't send a message so everyone assumed that he was ill. It wasn't like him to miss a performance but he had been getting quite tired lately so when he didn't show up I didn't really make much of it. I thought I'd leave him alone last night and go and see him this morning. He was such a lovely man, although he could be a little awkward at times.'

'And did you?'

'Did I what?'

Bartlett coughed and looked impatiently at Boase.

'Did you go and see him this morning?'

'Well, I tried. I went to his caravan and knocked a couple of times but there was no answer so I just thought he was still asleep.'

'And what time was that?'

'Oh, about midday, I suppose.'

'Was that normal for him to be still asleep at midday – did you not find that unusual?'

'Well, not really. We perform late sometimes and quite often we're late risers.'

'That makes sense, I suppose. Were you aware of anything that was troubling him or anyone who might have reason to harm him?'

Chester Martin sat back further in his chair.

'Harm him? Are you saying someone killed him?'

'I think that might be likely, sir.'

'But that's terrible. I ... I can't believe it.'

Bartlett stood up and went towards the door of the caravan. He turned and looked again at Chester Martin.

'I will need someone to identify Clicker – I understand from our previous enquiries here that he has no family – so, I would like to ask you if you can identify the body. Would you be able to do that for us, sir?'

'What do you mean ... no family?'

'Well, just what I say. That's what I understand to be the case.'

'It isn't true. He has a daughter.'

'And where might I find her?'

'Here.'

'*Here?*'

'Yes. Clicker's daughter is Molly James, the trick pony rider. I thought you must know that.'

'No. No, I didn't. Well, in that case, I will need to speak to her – along with the other members of the troupe.'

'Yes, of course. Please let me know if I can help in any way ... if there's anything you need?'

'I will. Thank you, Mr Martin.'

Bartlett and Boase left the caravan and Bartlett stopped to light his pipe. Boase coughed a few times.

'That smell was terrible, sir. I thought I was

50

going to be sick.'

'Yes, I thought it was pretty unpleasant myself. What do you make of him, Boase?'

'Nothing so far, sir.'

'Me neither – yet.'

Bartlett and Boase walked on towards the big top to see if anyone was inside rehearsing their act. The tent was empty.

'Strange, Boase – I'd have expected someone to be in here getting ready for tonight.'

'Me too, sir. Why don't we try some of the caravans?'

'Right, come on. Let's see if we can find his daughter first.'

At one end of a small row of circus caravans stood a rather modern affair; a luxurious green caravan, with horses' heads painted along the sides. Next to it, on a patch of grass, stood four white ponies, tethered and grazing. The door of the caravan was open.

'We got lucky, Boase.'

Bartlett knocked at the open door. An argument was clearly going inside the caravan. Eventually a tall man with blond hair stuck his head through the doorway.

'Yes ... what do you want?'

Bartlett introduced Boase and himself.

'Are you Edward James, sir?'

'Yes – what of it?'

'May we please speak to your wife?'

'What about?'

'Please, sir – don't try to get involved. Is she in here?'

Bartlett, knowing perfectly well that Molly James

was inside the caravan, having just heard the argument, pushed past the man and went inside. Boase followed. Molly was sitting at a small table. She looked up. Her face was tear-stained.

'Are you Molly James?'

'Yes ... yes, I am.'

Bartlett put his hand on the woman's shoulder.

'I'm sorry to tell you, Molly, that we have some bad news. Your father has been found dead.'

'My father?'

'Yes. We know about Clicker and your mother. We know the story.'

Molly looked terrified.

'What story?'

'About your parents here in the circus – and you as a baby.'

The woman looked visibly relieved.

'Oh, that.'

'Did you understand what I just told you, Molly? About your father?'

'Yes. What happened to him?'

'Well, we're not entirely sure yet but it looks like he was murdered.'

'*Murdered?* Oh, that's terrible. Who could do such a thing?'

At this, Molly burst into tears again and held her head in her hands.

'That's one of the reasons I've come to see you – I thought you might have an idea of who could have done this.'

'But I haven't. No idea. Everyone loved my father – you only need to ask around here, they'll all tell you how much they thought of him.'

The woman continued to cry. Bartlett patted

her hand.

'We'll leave you now. I'm so sorry to bring you such awful news, truly I am. Now, please don't go anywhere because we will probably need to speak to you again ... and someone will come to ask you to identify your father's body; I'm so sorry but you are his next of kin.'

'I won't go anywhere.'

The two men left the caravan and walked a little way. Bartlett lit his pipe.

'Well?'

'They're a strange couple all right.'

'Why do you say that?'

'She was obviously distraught and he just stood there – no attempt to comfort her.'

'Well, some people are like that, Boase. And we'd just heard them having a big argument when we arrived. Did you catch any of that?'

'No, sir – only the curses.'

'Hmm – me too. So, where next?'

Chapter Four

Bartlett and Boase worked their way around the circus site, breaking the news of Clicker's death and trying to find out how much, if anything, everyone knew. By late afternoon they called a halt to the proceedings.

'They're all keeping their cards close, sir.'

'Maybe they genuinely don't know anything – no way of telling really. Now, the only people we haven't managed to speak to are the Warner girls. What time did that groundsman say they'd be back?'

'Half past five. It's nearly that now – shall we wait?'

'I think we should. One of them has to be the girl you saw with the old man that evening – they're the only females left that we haven't spoken to. Yes – we'll hang on.'

Bartlett and Boase sat on a wall and waited. Twenty minutes later, three young women walked through the gates of the recreation ground. Boase stood up and called out to them.

'Hello. Are you the Misses Warner?'

The girls walked across the grass and approached Boase. Betty spoke first.

'Yes, we're the Warners – I'm Betty, this is Joan and this is Anne. Can we help you?'

'I'm Constable Boase, this is Inspector Bartlett. Could we please speak to you about Clicker?'

Anne, the youngest of the girls, grabbed Boase's arm.

'Clicker? Have you seen him? Where is he? Is he all right?'

Boase immediately recognised Anne as the person he had seen with the clown the night he was at the circus.

'Have you seen him? Please tell me where he is.'

Bartlett looked at the young girl who had now begun to cry.

'I'm sorry, miss, we have some bad news about Clicker.'

'Oh, no, please, no.'

Joan stepped forward.

'What's happened, Inspector Bartlett? – my sister is very fond of him.'

'I have to tell you that Clicker has been found dead.'

At this news, Anne let out a wail and fell to the ground. Betty and Joan picked her up.

'I will need to speak to all three of you about this – is there somewhere we can talk?'

Joan pointed to a nearby caravan.

'That's ours – we can talk in there.'

The small group made the short walk to the little caravan and went inside.

Betty made tea for everyone.

'Here you are, Inspector Bartlett, Constable Boase.'

Bartlett sipped his tea and looked at Anne.

'It's obvious, Anne, that you were very fond of Clicker. Can you tell us a bit more about him? We've been to see his daughter but she was a little unhelpful. I'm coming back to see her to-morrow.'

'Oh, her. Well, she didn't *deserve* him as a father. *We* lost our parents in a fire – which is why we ended up here; we had nowhere else to go. She's a hateful and greedy woman, Inspector Bartlett.'

'What makes you say that, Anne?'

'Because I know her. Clicker told me every-thing was fine until she pitched up – of course he was so happy to see her. But then ... well, then she started to become demanding.'

'Demanding? About what?'

Anne began to cry again.

'What can you tell us, Anne? This is very im-portant.'

55

'I think this may be all *my* fault. Did he kill himself, Inspector?'

'No, we don't think he did. It doesn't look like it. Why do you think this is your fault?'

'Because it was me that told Clicker that she was a liar. It was to do with Molly's mother.'

Boase stood behind Bartlett with a notebook and pencil, scribbling down everything that Anne said.

'Go on.'

'Well, Clicker liked me a lot and I liked him – he was almost like a father to me. He used to tell me all his little secrets and stories about his life. Molly's mother was in this very circus, years ago. She was Margaret Field – they called her the most daring high wire act in the world.'

Bartlett looked round at Boase.

'I think I've heard about her – she was a Londoner, if I'm not mistaken. Yes, very famous she was. Go on, Anne.'

'Well, they had a relationship many years ago, she and Clicker, and Molly was born. For some reason, just a couple of months before the birth, Margaret ran away. She left a note for Clicker saying she wanted to get away and not to look for her. He was distraught. He loved Margaret so very much. Anyway, a couple of years ago, Molly James appeared with her husband. She told Clicker that her mother was in a sanatorium in Switzerland and that she had something wrong with her lungs. Clicker wanted to go and see her but Molly just said she was too ill. She also said that she was struggling to keep up with the medical bills and could Clicker help her out a little.

56

Well, naturally, he was happy to. But it never stopped. She just kept on taking more and more money from him – he barely had anything left, Inspector Bartlett. He felt that she wasn't capable of doing such a thing, he really believed that Edward, her husband was behind the extortion – that's what it was, Inspector, extortion.'

'So how is this all your fault?'

Anne looked at her sisters. Joan squeezed her hand.

'Go on, Anne dear. Tell Inspector Bartlett everything you know – for Clicker's sake.'

Anne dabbed her eyes with a handkerchief.

'I wasn't really prying but I just saw something in an old newspaper. When I get homesick and bored – which is often – I go to the reading room at the library on the moor. I was looking at some papers a few weeks ago and that's when I saw it – the article. I'm ashamed to say I stole it from the library. Look, here it is – am I in trouble now?'

Bartlett smiled.

'Well, we don't normally encourage stealing from libraries but, given everything that's happened, I think we can overlook it.'

Anne shook open the newspaper.

'Look, Inspector. It's an article which is seven years old – it's about Margaret Field.'

Bartlett reached into his inside coat pocket for his reading spectacles.

'Well, this says she died in 1917.'

'Yes – and Clicker has been paying vast sums of money to the Jameses ever since they turned up here. They knew she was dead – there never *was* any clinic in Switzerland! I'm not ashamed to say

57

that I showed this to Clicker the other evening. But I am sorry to say that now he's dead and it could be because of me.'

Boase flipped over another page in his notebook. As he did so, he gestured towards the wall outside.

'Were you talking to him just over there, before the performance?'

'Yes, that's right, I was. I showed him this. He got very upset and said I shouldn't have got involved. That was the last time I saw him.'

Anne buried her head in her hands and sobbed.

Bartlett patted the girl's shoulder.

'This isn't your fault, Anne – you must stop thinking like this immediately. We'll leave you now but we may want to speak to you again, if that's all right?'

Anne smiled a weak smile.

'Yes, of course that's all right – I'm sorry I couldn't be of more help.'

'You've been very helpful. Thank you, ladies. Goodbye.'

Two fairly uneventful days passed at the Falmouth police station, other than Clicker's body being positively identified by his daughter and some sketchy news about the break-in at the church. Bartlett had been asking for almost a year for his office to get a new coat of paint and so it was that at seven o'clock in the morning, two painters arrived and knocked at his door. Boase had come in early and he opened the door to them. The two men looked to be in their early sixties, one about five feet two, the other about six feet two. The taller man spoke first. Holding aloft a paint can, he gestured towards the office.

'Mornin' – Painter.'

'Well, yes, I can see that...'

'No, my name – I'm Peter Painter. This is my brother, Paul. We've come to do your office.'

Boase looked at the tall man and then at the short one. He held the door wide.

'You'd better come in – is this going to take long?'

Now the short man spoke.

'Well, sir – it's in a bad way. It'll need two coats, so probably one today and one tomorrow.'

'My chief isn't going to be happy about that – we've got work to do. Although he *has* been asking for this to be done for some time.'

'I'm sorry, sir, but you won't want to be in here once we get started – it'll get on your nerves. It's the smell you see, sir. We're used to it ourselves but, well, to those outside the trade, it can get a little unpleasant.'

At this, Bartlett entered the office.

'What's unpleasant? What's going on, Boase?'

Boase chuckled.

'Well, these are the Painters, sir.'

'I think I've worked that out, Boase. But I didn't expect them until next week.'

'Their *name* is Painter, sir – Peter and Paul.'

'Oh, right. Well, this is rather inconvenient – can't you come back next week?'

Paul propped the ladder he had been holding, against the wall.

'If we don't start today then we can't start at all.'

59

Bartlett flung his coat onto the back of his chair.

'Now look here...'

Boase stepped between Bartlett and Paul Painter.

'Sir, you did say you wanted it done – and you have been waiting such a long time. We will probably be even busier next week with everything that's going on.'

Bartlett saw the logic in Boase's statement and agreed.

'All right – but you must work as quickly as possible. No standing around drinking tea all day. We're busy people and we need our office.'

The door reopened and Constable Penhaligon stuck his head into the office.

'Sorry to interrupt, sir. Superintendent Greet has asked me to tell you that he's put you and Constable Boase in the small office just while the painting is being done. I've put a pot of tea in there for you both.'

Bartlett looked at Boase.

'Why can't we stay in here?'

'Apparently the smell will be quite bad, sir – come on, it's only for a couple of days.'

Bartlett collected his coat and a few things from his desk and he and Boase went out, crossed the hall and went into the small office.

Bartlett lit his pipe.

'Look at this, Boase – Coad and Eddy did a good job on that church case. If I'm honest, I didn't think they had it in them.'

Bartlett slid a pile of papers across the desk to Boase.

'Looks like it was a couple of delinquents – thought they'd break into the church and steal the silverware.

'Did you hear what happened, Boase?'

'No, I didn't. How did they catch them?'

'Apparently they were at one of the lads' houses – just making a routine enquiry. The boy was up-stairs with the window open and heard what was being said. He tried to run away – Coad heard him and sent Eddy round the back and they stopped him. He gave the other boy's name and they were both arrested – and they retrieved the stuff. They're going back to the church later to return it.'

'Good job, sir.'

'I'd say so – means we can get on with the big job without having that in the background. Talking of that, where are we on this murder now?'

'Well, I'm thinking that we should go back and talk to that Edward James – Anne said that he and Clicker didn't get on. She said that Clicker was firmly of the opinion that *he* was behind all the money-making racket ... but why would that make him a killer? Surely he would want to keep him alive, to get as much as possible out of him.'

Bartlett was listening and nodding.

'Yes, but, what if Clicker was running out of money? Didn't Anne say that he was finding it difficult to keep up with their demands?'

'But that's not really a motive for killing though, is it? What if Edward James knew that someone had told Clicker that Margaret Field was dead? Perhaps Clicker told him the game was up and he was coming to tell us ... that would mean Clicker would have to be stopped.'

'That's a very good point you make, Boase. We still need to look further afield for our man – or woman – but I agree, so far, that's a rational opinion.'

Boase spun round and round on the swivel chair that had been assigned to him.

'Will you stop that, Boase!'

'I'd love one of these, sir. Maybe I could pinch it and take it back to our office? No one would miss it – this room is hardly ever used.'

'You're so immature sometimes, Boase. You can take it but if you keep spinning like that all the time, I'm bringing it back.'

'Thanks, sir – that's a proper job, that is.'

Bartlett grunted.

'Will you pay attention ... listen, I agree that we need to speak to Edward James. Not least, we need to find out if he has an alibi. I think we'll go up there later and speak to a few more people. Chester Martin is furious that he's had to postpone his tour– reckons it'll cost him thousands. I told him that's too bad, none of them is leaving Falmouth until we resolve this.'

'Right, sir. They'll just have to put up with it. Come on, let's drink our tea and then we may as well go up there and see James.'

'Good idea – I'm sick of this pokey little office already. Drink up.'

At two o'clock, Bartlett and Boase walked up Killigrew and to the recreation ground to speak to Edward James. As they approached the caravan he shared with Molly, they both stopped. The sounds of shattering glass and shouting came from inside the caravan.

'That's them, Boase. They always seem to be arguing.'

Bartlett knocked on the door and, within seconds, Edward James stood on the step.

'You two again ... what is it now?'

'Mr James – may we come in?'

Molly looked up as the pair entered.

Bartlett cleared his throat.

'Mr James, I just wanted to ask you about your relationship with your father-in-law. Did you get on with him?'

'I tried – but he was a quite a difficult old man, you know. I always made an effort with him but I don't think he liked me very much.'

'And why might that be?'

'Who knows? Does it matter now?'

At this, Molly looked up at her husband.

'What are you talking about? You *never* liked him.'

'That's not fair, Molly – I did my best with him.'

Bartlett sat next to Edward.

'Mr James, I need to ask you where you were on the night that Clicker was killed.'

'You can't believe I had anything to do with it – you're ridiculous.'

'Just tell us where you were, and the name of someone who can attest to that, and we'll be on our way. Clicker was seen by my assistant here at about half past six that evening. Where were you for the rest of the evening and night?'

'Well, I was here for the performance – plenty of people saw me. After that I came back here, sorted out the ponies and went to bed.'

'And can anyone verify that?'

'My wife here can.'

'But can anyone else?'

'No, of course not – there's only the two of us living here.'

'Very well. I'm sorry to have troubled you both. Good afternoon.'

Bartlett paused at the hospital wall at the top of Killigrew and lit his pipe.

'Do you believe him, Boase?'

'Dunno, sir. What do we do if we can't find anyone to speak for his whereabouts? And who else are you thinking of as a possible killer?'

'I haven't got anyone at the moment – none of this makes any sense to me. As you pointed out, why kill someone who was giving you regular – and easy money? If you're right and it's Edward James then the only reason is that Clicker told him he knew about the con. Everyone says what a lovely man he was, a decent sort, so it doesn't fit that he had lots of enemies.'

'But we only need *one* enemy, sir.'

'Yes, my boy – you're right there. I was looking at that report this morning – it confirmed my earlier suspicions – definitely murder, no two ways. The body has been thoroughly examined and we've been over the scene. Yes, it's murder all right. There's no way he did that to himself.'

The two men made their way back down Killigrew and to the station. As Bartlett crossed the main hall to his temporary office, the desk sergeant stopped him.

'Excuse me, sir. Penhaligon took a telephone message for you about half an hour ago – he's had to go up to the Catholic church to see Canon Egan but he asked me to give you this.'

The sergeant handed a folded piece of paper to Bartlett who took it and followed Boase into the office. They both removed their coats and Bartlett read the note. He looked up at Boase.

'Who's Aitchinson?'

'Who?'

'Aitchinson – look, Penhaligon's writing isn't the best but that definitely says "Aitchinson", doesn't it?'

Boase grasped the piece of paper, squinted, then handed it back.

'Yes, I'd say so, sir.'

'Do we know anyone called Aitchinson?'

'Well, I don't. What does the note say? I only looked at the name.'

'It says Penhaligon spoke to this man on the telephone. The man said that he doesn't want any trouble but that he saw Edward James leave the circus and head for the seafront the night Clicker was killed. Apparently the Jameses were the second act on – is that right?'

'Yes, as I recall, yes they were. What else does it say?'

'Nothing much – but we don't know anyone at the circus called Aitchinson. Have we met everyone?'

'Yes, every last one, sir.'

'What time did the pony act finish? Can you remember?'

'Yes, I can. Irene looked at her watch because

65

she thought the act seemed over very quickly. She said she hoped the others would be a bit longer because she was enjoying herself so much. She said "Look, that's two acts finished and it's only ten to eight".'

'What time do they think Clicker was killed?'

'They said between nine o'clock and midnight – that was the closest they could say.'

'So if this here Aitchinson is telling the truth, Edward James could have gone after the old man and got back to his caravan fairly quickly.'

'I suppose so, sir.'

Bartlett pushed his chair back from the desk.

'But who *is* Aitchinson? Could it be someone not connected with the circus? We're assuming he's one of the troupe. He's left no other details. Penhaligon writes here that he didn't want to give a name at all until he was pressed.'

'So, it's possibly a false one, sir?'

'Would you think of "Aitchinson" on the spur of the moment? It's not a very common name, is it?'

'No – but maybe it's a name that means something to him – like his mother's maiden name or something. Or, maybe it *is* his real name and we just haven't come across him.'

'Well, we *need* to come across him – if this is true, it's vitally important that we speak to him. We have to start with the name he's given and try to find out about him. You can ask those layabouts out there to start on that.'

Bartlett was gesturing towards the main office where two constables had spent the morning trying to look invisible in order not to have to do anything.

'When you've done that, we must arrange to speak to anyone we haven't already spoken to and who live on the approaches to Hunter's Path. Maybe there's still someone who saw *something* that night. Get on to all that will you, Boase?'

'Of course, sir.'

'Oh, before I forget, Caroline and Irene were wondering if you'd like to come over this evening – Irene's got some new card games she wants to try out on us. Fancy it?'

'That'd be lovely, sir. I was thinking of calling on Irene to see if she'd like a walk later on anyway.'

'Good. Come over at about seven?'

Chapter Five

Irene dealt the cards out to the small group around the table: her parents, Boase, and herself.

Boase watched as the diamond engagement ring he had recently bought her flashed in the light of the parlour. He smiled to himself and, when Irene caught him, smiled at her. He had worried that she wouldn't like it – but he was wrong. Every night the ring was returned safely to its box on the bedside table and every morning the box was opened and Irene looked at it again. Now, as they were introduced to yet another new card game, Boase felt happy. He hated cards – ever since the long days and nights in the trenches when any spare moment not occupied with writing letters home

67

seemed to be spent in endless card games. No, Boase did not like card games – but, for Irene, anything.

Bartlett rose from his seat.

'I think I find it strange now.'

Caroline looked at him.

'What's strange, George?'

'Well, that I still call this young man – soon to be my son-in-law – "Boase".'

'Well, that *is* my name, sir.'

'*And* that you call me "sir". I think we shall have to stay as we are at work but, other than that, I will call you "Archie" – if that's all right with you?'

'Of course it is.'

'And you – well, what do you think, Princess?'

George Bartlett looked at his wife.

'I did say before, George, that Archie should perhaps call you "George".'

'Well, that *is* my name – yes. "George" it shall be. That's that sorted then. Would you like a Leonard's, Archie?'

'Yes, I would, please ... George.' Boase felt uncomfortable with this arrangement but knew things had to change now.

Bartlett handed over a bottle of his beloved Leonard's London Beer and a glass.

'Here you are – why don't we sit in the comfortable chairs – I've had enough of cards for now, Irene.'

'All right, Dad. I'll put them away – I'm just going to make some tea for Mum and me.'

Bartlett and Boase sat by the fire and Topper sat on the floor between them.

'I can't believe that we still light a fire at this

time of the year, my boy – but Caroline feels the cold rather a lot and I don't want her to be uncomfortable.'

'I think it's rather nice, sir – I mean, *George*. I like a nice fire.'

Boase looked into the flames.

'Do you think there'll be another war, sir?'

'I hope not, my boy. I certainly hope not. And I don't believe there will be – surely we've learned something after the last lot. Maybe in the distant future but not in my lifetime. They've got to leave time to find something else to get worked up about. I hope you never see the likes of that again – nor your children, should you have any.'

'I'm not so sure. I hope you're right but people are always fighting, aren't they? And who knows what sort of new modern world is waiting for us?'

'Well, I'm quite happy with the old one – the modern one can wait until I've gone. Now, where's my tobacco?'

Irene brought in a tray and laid it on the table. Caroline had been listening to the conversation and was glad when it ended. Losing a son to the last war was more than any mother should have to bear and she certainly never wanted Irene to experience the distress that she herself had gone through with their son, John.

Bartlett had found his tobacco and now sat happily with his pipe and his beer. He looked at Boase.

'That's a queer business with that clown, right enough. I don't know where to begin and no error.'

'I can't believe that someone would kill that

69

poor old man, Dad. Archie and I were looking forward to seeing him at the circus. Why would anyone do something so horrible? I was reading about it to Mum from the *Packet*. It's terrible.'

'Yes, it is, Irene. Archie and I have got our work cut out there. But we'll find out what happened; we'll find out who killed the old man.'

Eleven o'clock came all too quickly for Boase and he reluctantly had to leave. Leaving was something he hated doing whenever he was with Irene but it wouldn't be forever. With that thought firmly in his head, he said his goodbyes and left for home.

'Any news on Aitchinson?

Bartlett addressed the desk sergeant and a constable as soon as he came through the front door of the police station. By now, everyone there had heard about the note and the mysterious Mr Aitchinson. The sergeant shook his head.

'Sorry, sir. We were on it all afternoon yesterday but nothing so far.'

'Keep looking – we need to know. It's urgent.'

Boase was already in the temporary office and had made Bartlett and himself some tea.

'Morning, sir. Cuppa?'

'I wouldn't say no – thank you, Boase. What's that there?'

'Oh, just a pork pie, sir – want a piece?'

'Well – no, because that is not breakfast, but I was rather referring to the piece of paper *under* the pie.'

'Oh this?'

Boase slid the paper out and showed it to

Bartlett. It had one word written on it:

AITCHINSON

'Go on.'

'Well, nothing really – I was just playing with the name. I even wondered if it was an anagram. But it isn't. I was just looking at it again while I was having a snack and waiting for the tea to brew.'

'I had hoped you were going to tell me something incredible but true and we'd be arresting the killer by lunchtime.'

'Sorry, sir.'

Bartlett laughed and sipped his tea.

'Are we sure Penhaligon heard him correctly?'

'Yes. I asked him again – that's definitely what he heard.'

'Accent?'

'None that he could discern – not local, not anything really, he thought.'

'Why would the caller want to incriminate Edward James – is it someone who has had some past dealings with him?'

'Maybe it's just the truth, sir, and the caller is doing his civic duty but without wishing to involve himself any further.'

'But by being covert, it makes it appear *untrue*, don't you think?'

'I don't know what to think at the moment. Come on, sir, drink your tea while it's still hot.'

Bartlett complied and stared out of the window.

'Can we move back in today, Boase? There's

71

nothing to see out of this window – I miss my own view.'

'Yes, we can go back in after lunch apparently, sir.'

Boase swivelled on his new chair and took another bite from his pork pie.

At the recreation ground, everyone was miserable, particularly Chester Martin who wasn't making any money. Superintendent Greet had forbidden the troupe to leave the town. However, he *had* given them permission to continue with their shows. Apart from the recent events putting a dampener on everything within the circus, the people of Falmouth had obviously decided that they wanted nothing more to do with it. And so it was that Chester Martin reluctantly pasted a sign outside saying that there would be no more performances in the town.

Anne Warner hadn't been able to sleep. She had lain in bed all night getting more and more angry, tired and upset. Now morning, she turned and looked at the small alarm clock beside the bed. It was half past ten. She was usually up and about by now but today she didn't feel like it. She really missed her dear friend, Clicker. She sat up and wondered why anyone would do something like that. He was such a lovely man. She'd bet any money that his daughter had something to do with this. *Clicker must have told her that he knew about Margaret Field.* And what of Edward James? *He never liked Clicker* – the old man had told her so many times that the two didn't get along.

Clicker just put up with him for the sake of being close to his daughter. He had waited for years to see her for the first time and had been prepared to do anything to keep her in his life – yes, even so far as to give her all his money.

Anne got up and made some tea. Her sisters had left a note propped up against the mirror saying they'd gone shopping and didn't want to wake her. She had been awake and heard them go but didn't feel like striking up a conversation with them. They meant well and they both loved her very much but, at the moment, she wanted to be alone with her thoughts. To the two older sisters, she had seemed to be so upset and tired over the last couple of days and they were growing more worried for her.

Anne drew her dressing gown tighter and sipped her tea. She hadn't eaten anything, *couldn't* eat anything. She felt hungry but didn't want anything. The last time she had felt like this was when her parents died – and Clicker had helped her to get over that a little. Now she was going through it all over again. As she watched the rain trickling down the caravan window, she saw someone hurrying across the grass. She looked closer. The woman was holding a raincoat over her head. As she watched, the figure disappeared from her sight. Seconds later there was a knock at the door. Anne rose and went to see who it was. As she opened the door, a gust of wind blew over a small vase on a nearby shelf. She pushed the door further and was surprised to see Molly James standing there. This was someone she liked less now than she had before.

Molly seemed far from pleased to see Anne. She spoke first. 'I was wondering if Betty or Joan were in?'

'No. They're not. What do you want?'

'They said before just to look in if I needed anything.'

The woman was holding a small jug.

'Milk?'

'If you can spare any – Edward hasn't had a cup of tea yet. He's going mad because I forgot to get milk yesterday.'

'You'd better come in – I do have some.'

'Thank you.'

The woman removed the coat from her head, shook it outside and came in. She looked uncomfortable and so did Anne, who worked quickly to fill the jug, spilling some of it onto the counter. Molly glanced around the small caravan, trying to avoid looking at the girl. The jug was filled and handed back.

'Thanks – you're very kind.'

No reply was offered as the door was opened, and the woman hurried back out into the rain. Anne felt shaky and sat to finish her tea. She took a biscuit from the tin but after only a small bite threw it down on the table. She wished her sisters would hurry up. She didn't like being alone here now.

Bartlett and Boase finished putting everything back into their newly painted office, including Boase's recently acquired swivel chair, which he ceremoniously placed behind his desk with a satisfied grin. Bartlett stared at him.

'Are you just going to stare at it, or actually sit in it to do some work?'

'Well, sir, much as I'd love to sit in my new chair, I was thinking about going back to the circus to see if I could speak to anyone else – I'm sure there's something obvious we've missed. I need to know about Aitchinson. I've asked Penhaligon again if he can remember anything else but he says everything the man said to him, he wrote down. I thought, if it's all right with you, I'd go up there and then go straight home – unless you need me to come back?'

'Well, no, and I haven't got any better ideas. I've got to go up and see Greet in a minute or two, so if you think you'll be more use doing that, then you go ahead.'

'Righto, sir. I'll just finish this piece of cake and I'll be on my way.'

Boase didn't go straight to the recreation ground. Instead he went into the town. He never took a proper break but he thought he'd have half an hour now so that he could collect a gift he'd reserved for Irene, just to remind her that he loved her. He walked through the streets until he came to Bendix and Hall, the jewellers in Arwenack Street. He entered and waited his turn. There was a rather stout woman in front of him.

'Mr Bosustow – this is not up to the usual high quality service my husband and I have come to expect from you. Now, did I tell you that my husband bought this ring from Hatton Garden – that's in London you know – especially for our fortieth wedding anniversary? That is tomorrow. I expected to have this alteration done by today

75

and now you tell me it is not ready. I am very distressed, Mr Bosustow. Very distressed indeed.'

Boase smiled and felt rather sorry as Mr Bosustow drew himself up to his full height of about five feet six inches and addressed the woman looming over him.

'Mrs de Vere, in the first place, quite obviously, I know where Hatton Garden is. Madam, I am a jeweller. In the second place, I told you perfectly well that your ring would be altered and ready for collection tomorrow. May I have your receipt docket please?'

Mrs de Vere rummaged through a voluminous handbag and presented the man with a yellow slip of paper. He unfolded it and held it up in front of her face and said merely one word.

'Look.'

Mrs de Vere did indeed look and now began to speak very quickly.

'Well, of course, you see it's your dreadful handwriting; shocking, that's what it is.'

'Maybe your eyesight is not what it used to be, madam. I also would not have told you to collect today as I only have two repair days each week. Now, if you would like to return tomorrow, you may collect your ring at nine o'clock, if that would suit?'

Mrs de Vere was now reversing out of the shop and bumped into Boase who had been looking at some watches in a cabinet. He touched his hat. She made a small attempt at a curtsy and left the shop. Quentin Bosustow brushed the front of his coat and returned to his place behind the counter.

'Good day, Mr Boase. How are you?'

76

'Good afternoon, Mr Bosustow, looks like you had your hands full there.'

'Well, Mrs de Vere is a very good customer and has been for more years than I care to remember. However, she can be, shall we say, just a little trying.'

Boase smiled.

'Have you come to collect your necklace?'

'Yes, please. This is really very kind of you.'

'Well, my father-in-law started the practice of instalments and I could see no reason to discontinue. Not all of my customers have unlimited means and why should they be deprived of a little luxury?'

'Quite, Mr Bosustow.'

The jeweller unlocked a drawer underneath the counter and withdrew a small brown envelope. He laid the contents onto a blue velvet pad.

'This is such a pretty necklace, Mr Boase. I just know your fiancée will be extremely happy with it. Are emeralds a favourite of hers?'

'Well, she has green eyes...'

'Oh, well then this will be just perfect. Wait a moment and I'll put it in a box for you. How about a green one?'

'Thank you, Mr Bosustow.

'Now, let me sign your receipt and you can be on your way.'

The business concluded, Boase left the shop and headed towards the recreation ground, sporadically touching his pocket to make sure his precious cargo was still aboard.

Having left the jeweller's and wanting the most direct route to the recreation ground, Boase had walked up Swanpool Street, along Woodlane and was now going along Western Terrace. As he reached the Observatory he saw someone running along the pavement on the opposite side of the road. He looked again and recognised Anne Warner. She was crying. Boase crossed over and ran up to her.

'Miss Warner? Anne – it's me, Archie Boase. Are you all right, Anne?'

Anne collapsed against the wall.

'Oh, Constable Boase. Thank you. No, I'm not quite myself, I'm sorry.'

'Where are you running to?'

'I was looking for my sisters. They went out without me and then Molly James came over for some milk because her husband was angry with her and my sisters haven't come back and then Edward James came and just opened my door and walked in. He was really shouting at me saying I was rude to his wife – I think he must have been drinking and, oh! I hate that horrible circus. I'm so frightened. I want my friend Clicker back.'

Anne stopped talking and began to cry again. Boase put his arm around her.

'Come on, I was just coming to your place. I'll take you back. I'm sure your sisters will be back in a minute. Where have they gone?'

'Shopping I think.'

'Oh, well, there you are then. Just like my fiancée, Irene – she loves shopping. I'm sure they won't be long though. Let's cross here, shall we?'

As they headed toward the Warner caravan, Betty and Joan were waiting outside. Boase pointed to them.

'There you are, Anne. Told you they wouldn't be long.'

The two sisters took Anne and Boase into the caravan and Anne explained what had happened.

'I think your sister's still in shock – she needs a strong cup of tea.'

'You're right, Constable Boase. Will you join us?'

Betty was filling the kettle.

'No, thank you. I just wanted another look around here and then I've finished for the day.'

'Will you catch whoever killed Clicker?'

Anne was drying her eyes with a handkerchief.

'We'll do our very best, Anne. I promise you that. I should be going. If any of you hear any news, be sure to let me know, will you? 'Bye then.'

Boase had another look around the site. There were very few people around and no one had anything to tell him that was new. He wondered why Anne had got so upset about Edward James but could see from the treatment of his wife that the man could be very intimidating. He went and knocked on the door of the Jameses' caravan but there was no reply. Boase felt irritated – he wanted to see why this man was now bullying Anne. He wandered around a bit longer, petted the ponies which were tied up by the caravan and then took the decision to come back tomorrow with a better plan.

Anne Warner couldn't sleep. She didn't want to wake her sisters, so she quietly got up and poured herself a glass of water. It wasn't a particularly warm night, but Anne had been turning over and over in her bed, recent events rattling around inside her head and she had felt uncomfortably hot. She sat quietly beside the window and drew back the curtain. The moonlight lit up the inside of the small caravan. She finished two glasses of water but felt no better. It was as though she couldn't breathe properly. As she went to put the empty glass in the sink, it fell from her hand with such a noise it seemed to echo loudly around the caravan. She began to pick up the biggest pieces and, as she did so, a light came on in the bedroom. The door opened and Betty stood there hastily wrapping her dressing gown around herself.

'What's happened, Anne? Why are you up at this hour?'

'I ... I couldn't sleep and now I've broken a glass. I feel very hot and a little shaky.'

'Let me feel your head, dear. Anne – you're practically on fire.'

The older Warner girl pushed open the door of the caravan and told Anne to sit on the step.

'I'll get you a cool flannel. Wait here.'

Betty sat on the step with Anne for five minutes then, stifling a yawn, stood up.

'Well, I don't know about you but I'm exhausted. Are you feeling any better now?'

'I've cooled down a bit, thanks.'

'I'm off to bed, Anne dear, it's almost two. Are you coming?'

'I think I'll just sit here a little longer, if that's all right?'

'Of course, but don't be too long; you look very tired. Goodnight, Anne.'

''Night, Betty.'

Anne remained on the step, looking up at the bright moon and thinking about her dear old friend, Clicker. She thought about her parents and how much she missed them. As she was about to get up, she thought she heard a sound just across the grass. She listened. Nothing now. It must be her imagination; she *was* very tired, after all. As she rose, she saw a shadow darting across between the caravans opposite her own. It was clearly a person running swiftly. Anne stared harder then became afraid. After what had happened to Clicker, who knew what might happen next? She ran quickly inside the caravan and bolted the door.

Chapter Six

Edward James put the *Falmouth Packet* onto the table and picked up his knife and fork.

'Have you read this, Molly? It says the police are looking for anyone who was near Hunter's Path the night Clicker was killed. Well, they needn't look at me, I wasn't there. Blast it, Molly, do we *have* to have eggs every day? Why can't we have a bit of bacon once in a while?'

'Because bacon costs money and that doesn't go far, that's why. It looks like old man Martin isn't going to pay us again – that's twice now. Reckons, with the show off, he just can't afford it and that the police won't let us leave until they're satisfied that no one here had anything to do with the murder.'

'Well, we can't go on, with no money. Have you got anything left from your father?'

'About two pounds ten.'

'Is that all – what the hell have you been doing with it?'

Edward rose from his chair, knife in hand. Molly stepped back.

'Stop it, Ed, you're frightening me. I've been as careful as I can with the money – it's not easy when there's nothing coming in. Please sit down and eat your breakfast. Here you are, here's a nice cup of tea.'

Trembling, Molly put the cup on the table. She had never been afraid of anyone in her younger days but since she met her husband, well, he could be very frightening when he was in a temper. She shouldn't have to be afraid. She took a little money from a jug under the sink.

'Look, we haven't completely run out of money – why don't I go to the shop and get a nice bit of bacon for your breakfast tomorrow?'

'Come here.'

'What? What for?'

'I said, come here.'

She walked towards him and he pulled her onto his lap. He kissed her.

'Stop it, Ed, don't be silly let me go.'

'I really love you, Molly. Why are you so on edge lately? You know I didn't have anything to do with your father being killed, don't you?'

'Course I do. Now let me go to the shop. I shan't be long.'

Edward watched his wife through the window

and sat back down to finish his breakfast.

Bartlett called Constable Penhaligon into his office.

'Penhaligon, is there any news of this Aitchinson character?'

'I'm really sorry, sir, no there isn't. We've tried everything we can think of.'

The door opened and Boase walked in.

'Morning, sir, morning, Penhaligon – am I interrupting something?'

'No, come in, Boase. I was just asking Penhaligon about our mysterious Mr Aitchinson. Greet nearly had a stroke this morning shouting at me. He's going too far but I suppose he has a point – Aitchinson is all we have to go on. No one saw anything near Hunter's Path that night, there's really no one else to ask. I'm stumped. Carry on, Penhaligon.'

Bartlett turned back to Boase.

'You any further forward on this, Boase?'

Boase was laying open a large napkin on his desk to reveal two ham sandwiches. He rubbed his hands together in anticipation.

'BOASE!'

'Sorry, sir, didn't have time for breakfast. I went to the recreation ground last evening but nothing doing. Although I did see Anne Warner in a state running along Western Terrace. I had to take her back to the caravan. She was in a right panic.'

'Did she say why?'

'Well, I think it's just the shock of everything. She's quite a timid little creature and very young. I think it all got on top of her. I left her with her sisters, anyway. I don't know what next, sir.'

'Do you think this has all come from within the circus, or outside, Boase?'

'If I'm honest, I *do* think it's on the inside – but at the moment I can't even tell you why.'

'Well, your hunches are usually fairly reliable. We're just going to have to go back again, and keep going back until this is sorted, or before Greet has a heart attack.'

'Want to go now, sir?'

'Yes. Hurry up with that sandwich and we'll be off, catch them nice and early. Get a car, will you, I'm shattered.'

The two men knocked at a few caravans and spoke to some of the troupe but the story was just the same; Clicker was a lovely old man, why would anyone want to kill him? and no, they hadn't seen anything or anyone suspicious.

'I just don't understand this, Boase. When someone is murdered in a little place like this, there's always someone who knows something, however small. It's not like when I was in London – that was a real big job, although I suppose there were more people closer together, all snooping.'

Boase couldn't help laughing at the vision he had conjured up, of lots of nosy Londoners all spying on each other.

'Do you miss it, sir? Being in London?'

'Some aspects I do, others not at all. The air is so clean and lovely here. But, of course, the most important thing, my Caroline. I think if we'd stayed in London she might not even still be here. Yes, I think she'd be gone by now with her illnesses.

She's so much better now and no error. Indeed, I'd do anything to see her well and she really loves it here, I can tell.'

Bartlett lit his pipe and looked at Boase.

'Did you hear what I just said?'

His constable was staring into the distance.

'Boase, what are you thinking about?'

'We spoke to Howard Smith and his son, Gregory – the fire-eaters – didn't we?'

'Twice.'

'Then how could we be so stupid!'

'Boase?'

'Sir, what do they call themselves – the fire-eaters?'

'I don't know. Fire-eaters?'

'No – look over there on that caravan.'

Boase was pointing to a small caravan a few yards away. It had the door open.

'I don't see what you're looking at – *or* what you're talking about, my boy.'

Boase was already running towards the caravan. The writing visible one the door read '*& Son*'. Boase, reaching the caravan, with Bartlett close behind him, slammed the door shut to reveal the words '*H & Son*'.

'Look, sir. Howard is 'H' so he and Gregory are 'H and Son' – AITCHINSON!'

'Well, I'll be...'

Boase was already hammering on the side of the caravan.

Howard Smith opened the door.

'What on earth is going on here? What's the meaning of this, banging on my caravan like a maniac?'

85

Boase spoke hurriedly.

'You're Aitchinson. You telephoned the police station about Edward James. Do you really think we're that stupid? It was only a matter of time. Go inside please, Mr Smith.'

Bartlett and Boase sat with the fire eater inside the caravan. Boase felt so angry with himself and with this man.

'Tell us why you made the call and what you know.'

'Well, I made the call to give you information because the sooner this murder is solved the sooner we can get on with our lives and start earning money. You know Chester Martin isn't paying us? Well, none of us can afford to live – one or two here have no savings and are practically starving. Gwynfor Evans especially – he's supposed to be the strongman. He can't afford to buy the amount of food he needs. He's completely run out of money. We can't all carry on like this and you police are worse than useless. You need to arrest Edward James and let us get on with our lives.'

Bartlett leaned forward in his seat.

'What do you mean we need to arrest Edward James? Why would you say that?'

'It's obvious he did the old man in. He hated him. He's a nasty piece of work. His own wife is terrified of him. And another thing, he's got a gun. He doesn't need one. The only people here who need a gun are the lion tamers – and they've got rifles. James has a pistol, I've seen it.'

'When did you see the gun?'

'He sits on the step cleaning it. I think he does it to keep his wife in line.'

'So, what real evidence do you have?'

The fire eater raised his voice.

'It's just as I told your man – I saw Edward James going towards the seafront that night. He probably had the gun with him.'

Boase became agitated.

'Mr Smith, you've already wasted many hours of police time, making up that fictional name, and now you're making unfounded accusations.'

'Well, go and get his gun then. I bet you'll find it's the same one that killed the old man. In fact, you probably won't find it at all – he'll have dumped it, if he's got any sense.'

Bartlett and Boase got up from their seats. As they went through the door, Bartlett turned.

'Make sure you come into the station today. At three o'clock. You'll be making a statement regarding what you saw – or what you thought you saw. Don't be late.'

With the same thought in both their minds, Bartlett and Boase went immediately to the Jameses' caravan. Bartlett knocked at the door. It was opened by Edward James.

'Not you again!'

'We'd like to search this caravan, Mr James.'

'Well, you can't. I don't want you here upsetting my wife.'

Bartlett was becoming exasperated. 'Is your wife in?'

'No.'

'Well then, we won't be upsetting her.'

The two men pushed their way into the caravan and began their search. Ten minutes later, Boase called from the bedroom.

'It's here, sir!'

Edward James lunged towards Boase, who was holding up a gun.

'What are you doing? That's my property. You haven't even got a warrant.'

Bartlett turned to the man.

'I have my Superintendent's authority to search.'

'Well, let's just say we'd like to borrow it for analysis in connection with a murder investigation. In the meantime, get your coat, you're coming with us. We think you might have more to tell us.'

'Am I under arrest?'

Bartlett drew his pipe from his pocket and looked at Edward James.

'No, but it can be arranged. Coming?'

The suspect thought better of speaking again and went along with no further fuss.

Their suspect being held in a cell, Bartlett and Boase were told to give him a couple of hours to calm down before they spoke to him again. He had become very agitated and tried to punch Constable Penhaligon, who was fortunately rather too quick for the older man.

Bartlett looked out of the window.

'Do you think it's him?'

'Dunno, sir. We'll have that gun analysed – if that's different from the murder weapon then we might have a problem. But, aside from that, why else would he do it? Firstly, he didn't like the old man – not much of a reason. Second, the old man was giving the Jameses money, so why kill him? Third, until we speak to him, we don't know much else. I've asked for a police report from Halifax. I found out he was convicted of an assault there about eight years ago. Spent some time in prison for it.'

'Well done, Boase. How did you find out that?'

'I have ways, sir.'

Boase grinned and ate a hard-boiled egg which he had just rediscovered in his pocket.

Bartlett watched in amazement.

'I wondered what the smell was. How long have you had that in your pocket?'

'Only since yesterday, I think, sir.'

'God – you're going to poison yourself one of these days. I don't fancy my daughter being a young widow.'

Boase chuckled and finished his egg. He intended to have a bath when he got home. He was going to see Irene tonight and surprise her with the necklace. He certainly didn't want to be smelling of stale food when he held her close and kissed her.

At four o'clock, Edward James had still not calmed down enough to be interviewed and Superintendent Greet had been down to the cell to speak to him. This did nothing but further agitate the man and the door was locked until he submitted. Howard Smith had come in at three o'clock, as instructed by Bartlett, but had said nothing more in his statement than he had already stated earlier.

Bartlett came into his office and looked at Boase who was writing at his desk.

'Guess what?'

'What, sir?'

'Greet wants to interview Edward James. Thinks *he's* the best person to handle him.'

'But he's an idiot ... oh, sorry, sir...'

'Well, I can't argue with that. Anyway, he wants me there but says you're to go home. Sorry, my boy, but he's adamant on this. Is there anything you want me to ask or to say to him?'

'Not really, sir – you're more of an expert than me.'

As they spoke there was a knock at the door and the desk sergeant entered.

'Sorry to interrupt but it looks like your gun expert is working overtime – here's his report.'

Bartlett took the brown envelope and ripped it open. He read the single sheet of paper which had been inside.

'Blimey.'

'What, sir?'

'Boase, the gun had one bullet missing and it's exactly the same type that killed Clicker.'

'Well, *now* do you think it's James?'

'Well, it's fairly damning – unless ... I suppose someone could have stolen the gun and replaced it afterwards ... like Molly?'

'I don't think so – although she's a liar, I don't think she's a killer. As we said before, she was getting money from Clicker so why should she want that to stop – and he was still her father, after all. That's got to count for something surely?'

'But we don't know if Clicker had told her that he knew about Margaret Field. I don't want to bring it up yet until we know more. He had only just found out himself that same evening. I don't

90

understand all this, sir. Unless...'

'Unless Howard Smith was something to do with it.'

'Well, he's not saying much. We could speak to him again if you like.'

'Maybe, sir.'

'I've got to see Greet now and speak to James. You get off home. You seeing Irene later?'

'Yes, I am – I'm looking forward to it.'

'You cut along then. I might see you tonight then?'

'You might – 'bye, sir. Wish I was coming in with you.'

'So do I, Boase. So do I.'

Boase was sorry, yet not. He might have been stuck in a cell with Edward James for half the evening and then been late for Irene. Now, he could clean himself up, have time for a proper shave and be on time to see his fiancée.

Topper heard Boase opening the garden gate and ran to the front door, barking loudly. Irene came running down the stairs and, pulling Topper out of the way, opened the door. She pushed a stray wisp of hair back from her forehead.

'Hello, Archie – my word, you're early.'

'I'm so sorry, Irene.'

'I didn't say it was a problem – I'm always happy to see you, you know that.'

Irene reached up on tiptoe and kissed Boase's cheek. In return he kissed her lips.

'Well, let's not stand here, Archie. Come in. Dad's not back yet.'

'I know. He asked me to tell you that he might

be quite late this evening. Greet has asked him to stay with him to interview someone.'

Caroline Bartlett stuck her head around the parlour door.

'Good evening, Archie. Did I hear you say George will be late?'

'Yes, Mrs Bartlett ... er ... Caroline. Sorry. Yes, Superintendent Greet has asked him to stay.'

'You mean *told* him to stay. That man really has the limit of my patience. George does so much at that place and Greet takes advantage at every opportunity. Anyway, at least you're here. Come in and have some food.'

The three, accompanied by Topper, went into the dining room and sat at the table.

'I don't suppose there's any point waiting for your father, Irene. Goodness only knows what time he'll be back. I really don't like to eat without him. In fact, why don't you two go ahead and I'll eat later when he comes home?'

'Oh, Mum. You must be hungry. Have a little something to eat.'

'No, really, dear. I think I'll sit in the parlour; I have a little sewing I want to finish anyway. I'd rather wait and I'm sure you two have things to talk about. Look, I'll pour myself a cup of tea and take it into the other room. Help yourself to food, Archie. I know you're always hungry. Come on now, both of you – take as much as you like.'

Caroline took her tea into the parlour, leaving the couple alone.

'They love each other so much, Archie. She never eats anything when Dad's not here. Do you think we'll be like that one day?'

'I feel like it now, Irene. I really love you.'

'But I bet you don't stop eating when I'm not around. I don't think that would ever happen.'

Irene giggled and Boase scowled.

'Don't make fun of me, Irene – I have enough of your father going on about how much I eat.'

'I'm only teasing, Archie. Here, have some ham – I bet you're starving.'

Boase pulled Irene's chair closer to his and held her hand.

'I've brought you a present.'

'Archie – you're supposed to be saving your money. You don't need to be buying things for me all the time.'

'I don't do it all the time and anyway, this one is a special gift to remind you how much I love you.'

Boase took the green velvet box from his pocket and handed it to Irene. She took the box and opened it. At once a tear came to her eyes.

'What's the matter – don't you like it? I can change it for something else if you prefer.'

'Archie, I love it. It's so beautiful.'

'Not as beautiful as you.'

'But this must have been so expensive. I love it. Help me to put it on. Can I go and show Mum?'

Irene kissed Boase and ran into the parlour.

'Well, Topper, I think she likes it.'

Topper let out a sigh and surveyed the piece of ham that had earlier fallen into Boase's lap.

By ten o' clock there was still no sign of Bartlett and Caroline had fallen asleep in the chair. Boase said goodnight to Irene and left for home.

Chapter Seven

Two days had passed uneventfully and Bartlett and Boase were feeling despondent. Greet had gone behind their backs and found further evidence against Edward James.

'I think Greet should have let him go, Boase.'

'But you've seen the evidence, sir.'

'Patchy, my boy, patchy. I've just got a bad feeling about all this. I know you're right and I'm probably not thinking straight but I'd feel better if we had a better grip on all this.'

'Well, we don't know why Clicker was murdered but it's over now. Greet's got his man.'

'Well, there's the rub. I'm not convinced.'

'Cheer up, sir. Something's bound to turn up soon.'

'Yes, but we're running out of time – I don't want that London mob here snooping about in our business.'

Greet had always made it quite clear to Bartlett that if he didn't tie up a serious case within three days then he would call in the police from London to take over. Bartlett had always managed to avoid this in the past but now he was worried that his time was up. He certainly didn't want to be undermined and made to look incompetent. He'd have to do better than this. Greet was certain that James was the murderer yet Bartlett thought there was more to it than that. But *what?*

'Cuppa, sir?'

'I wouldn't say no – thought you'd never ask.'

As Boase opened the door, Penhaligon was on the other side with a tea tray.

'Good man – you read my mind. Thanks, Penhaligon.'

Penhaligon handed the tray to Boase and walked over to Bartlett's desk.

'Sir, I think you should know that Edward James has made a complaint – about the way he's been treated.'

'Oh, has he now?'

Bartlett looked at Penhaligon over the top of his glasses.

'Does Greet know?'

'Yes, sir. James wrote a letter directly to him. I can't say what was in it, sir. Superintendent Greet didn't say.'

'No doubt he'll be down here in a minute to tell all. Thanks, Penhaligon – and thanks for the tea.'

Bartlett took his cup from the tray and looked up at Boase.

'Can't say I blame him. Yes, he's violent to his wife and he's got a record for assault but that doesn't make him a killer, does it?'

'Well, no.'

'Superintendent Greet has asked to see you, sir.'

Bartlett stared at the desk sergeant.

'But it's only half past seven – what's he doing in so early?'

'Not sure, sir, but he told me to make sure that you went straight up the minute you arrived.'

'Right – tell Boase where I am when he comes

in, will you?'

'Yes, of course, sir.'

Boase arrived ten minutes later, picking up Bartlett's newspaper from the front desk, together with the news of Greet's meeting. He went into the shared office and hung up his coat.

'Penhaligon – Penhaligon ... any chance of some tea, please? I'm sure Inspector Bartlett will be glad of one when he comes down.'

Penhaligon went off to boil the kettle, bumping into Bartlett on his way.

'That man is a lunatic, Boase.'

'What? What's happened, sir – why did he want to see you so early?'

'He's let Edward James go.'

'But I thought that's what you hoped he'd do?'

'Yes, but why does he keep messing around? He says he's been told by the "big cheese" to let him go.'

'Parsons?'

'Yes, Parsons – told Greet that he'd need more evidence.'

'But that's a good thing, surely?'

'Well, yes, yes it is. I just wish Greet would leave us alone to get on with things our way.'

At that, Penhaligon came in with a tray.

'Tea, sir?'

'I wouldn't say no, Penhaligon. Thank you.'

Bartlett and Boase sipped their drinks in silence as Boase ate a ham sandwich.

Bartlett lit his pipe.

'Now we'll have to find some *real* evidence. I'm going back up there on my way home today when

I've cleared this mountain of work here, and I'm going to go through every last one of them at that circus. I'm not going to rest until I find whoever did this – not least because Greet's determined to make me look like an idiot in front of all and sundry. I know what he thinks – he thinks I can't do the job. He's been trying to get rid of me for a long time now. Well, I'm having none of it. You can come with me if you like – I'll warn you though, I might be there some time.'

Boase didn't like the way Bartlett was thinking and, taking his tea, returned to his desk to finish a report. The day dragged on, seemingly endless until Bartlett stood up and put on his hat and coat.

'Come on, Boase, let's get out of here.'

The light was fading as Bartlett and Boase made their way up Killigrew Street and into the recreation ground. 'I was hoping to get here before now, Boase.'

'Yes but you didn't expect to be held up so late. Anyway, you're more likely to find everyone in at this hour.'

'Look, Boase, there's two of the sisters – the jugglers. I don't think we can get much more out of them, though.'

Boase agreed as they watched Betty and Joan Warner walk towards their caravan and enter. Within seconds a scream was heard which echoed around the circle of caravans and Joan came running out. Bartlett and Boase ran across to her. Boase grabbed her by the arms.

'Joan ... Joan. What's wrong? What's happened?'

The girl couldn't answer, so Boase left her and ran across to Bartlett, who had just entered the caravan. The two men saw Betty leaning over Anne, who was slumped on the floor. Blood was seeping through the blue scarf Anne wore wrapped around her neck. Betty picked her up and rested her head in her lap.

'Anne, Anne. Speak to me, Anne. Who did this to you?'

Anne moved her lips slowly and Betty leaned nearer to hear the words she was trying to utter. She couldn't make them out and looked up at Bartlett. Boase had pushed forward and was pressing a cloth against the girl's neck to halt the bleeding but he quickly realised he was losing this battle. Picking her up in his arms he ran out of the caravan and across the road to the hospital. The sisters followed, horrified at the trail of blood Boase was leaving behind him. Bartlett had also run outside but was looking around the caravan. He searched underneath but there was no one there. Going back inside, he opened every cupboard and checked under each bed. Nothing.

At the hospital, a blood-soaked Boase stood waiting while two doctors and two nurses tried to help Anne. Joan and Betty sat down and held hands, crying. Boase walked across to them.

'The nurse says she was lucky – she hasn't severed an artery. Did you see anyone as you came up to the caravan? Have you any idea of who could do this?'

Joan wiped her eyes and looked up at Boase.

'Well, I suppose it's probably the same person who killed Clicker, and everyone says that's Edward James. You had him at the police station and you let him go.'

Bartlett, already thinking along the same lines, had walked into the James caravan to find Edward asleep in a chair. He woke him up.

'What the hell is it now? You can't just walk in here.'

'Were you anywhere near the Warner caravan earlier on?'

'No. I've been here all day. It's not like there's any work is it – thanks to you.'

'Can your wife verify that?'

'She was here earlier on but she's gone out for some shopping. I must have fallen asleep – boredom does that to people.'

'Stand up, please'

'What?'

'You heard – get up.'

Edward James stood and Bartlett inspected his clothes. There was no blood. In fact, Bartlett thought he looked uncharacteristically clean. Anyone who had just done that to Anne Warner would be covered in her blood and there certainly hadn't been enough time to clean up. He left the caravan and walked across to the hospital. As he entered the corridor he saw a doctor talking to the Warner sisters. Boase was walking towards him.

'What's happening, my boy?'

'She's dead, sir.'

'*Dead?*'

'I can't believe it. When I rushed here with her, they said it didn't look too bad. She'd lost a lot of blood but that could be dealt with. They've just come out now and said her heart gave out. Must have been the shock of it. I feel terrible that I didn't do enough to save her.'

'You did more than anyone, Boase. Meantime, I've just been over to see James – sitting there, calm as you like – asleep when I first went in, in fact. He wouldn't have had time to clean up that amount of blood. And look at you – you'd better go home and sort out some clean things. I'll get a car to take you back.'

'It's not far, I can walk.'

'Not looking like that you can't. Who would do such a thing to a child like that?'

The Warner sisters were staring at Bartlett and Boase and then they turned away.

'They think it's my fault, sir.'

'Well, they shouldn't, because it's not. My word, Greet's going to have a field day with this. Come on, let's get you sorted out with a car.'

Bartlett stopped by the Warners.

'I'm so very sorry, truly I am.'

Betty scowled at him.

'Well, that's not much good now, is it? How many more people are you going to watch being killed? She was just a child, Inspector Bartlett.'

'I know. I'm so sorry.'

Joan was sobbing uncontrollably and just stared at Bartlett. Having no more words to offer, he left the girls to their grief and went to organise a lift for Boase.

'Did either of Anne Warner's sisters get anything of what she was trying to say, Boase?'

'No, sir. I asked Betty again but she hadn't been able to hear. Do you think the girl was saying who did it?'

'Well, we'll never know now.'

Boase walked along Western Terrace the next morning feeling hungry; he hadn't been able to eat anything at breakfast. This business had really upset him. Clicker, well, that was one thing. Clicker was an old man – although that didn't make it OK. But Anne, she was such a sweet young thing and what a sad, short life she'd had. Boase felt upset and, worse, responsible.

Sitting behind his desk, Bartlett lit his pipe and looked at the clock on the mantelpiece in his office. It was a quarter past seven. He hadn't slept and had been in since six.

Constable Penhaligon knocked at the door and stuck his head round it.

'Sorry to interrupt, sir, but Howard Smith is here. Says he wants to see you.'

'Oh, our "Mr Aitchinson"? Right, yes, I'll see him. Bring him in, Penhaligon.'

Howard Smith came in and Bartlett directed him to a chair.

'What brings you here, Mr Smith? Thought of something else?'

'I can't believe you've let him go. You know it was him.'

'Actually, we don't.'

'I told you I saw him going to the seafront. It was shortly before you say the old man was killed. And why don't you ask his wife? I bet she can't give him an alibi because he wasn't there. And now, that poor Warner kid has been murdered – who do you think did *that*? She'd be alive now if you'd kept him locked up.'

Bartlett sat back in his chair.

'Mr Smith, you can't go around pointing the finger at all and sundry without any evidence. Now, *is* there anything else you want to say?'

'Just put him away, that's all I'm saying. Put him away before you've got another murder on your hands.'

Howard Smith stormed out and slammed the door.

Boase walked into the lobby of the police station. He quietly opened the door of the office he shared with Bartlett and sat behind his desk.

'Morning, Boase. You all right?'

'Morning, sir. Not really.'

Bartlett sighed.

'I don't think James killed Anne, really I don't, Boase, but we should get him in again anyway – ask him if he knows anything and see if he can shed any more light on Clicker.'

'Righto, sir. I'll see to it – in fact I'll bring him in myself. But I don't think a history of violence, even with a conviction for it, will be enough.'

'But he's violent with his wife *and* he had the weapon. Take a car and bring him in, Boase. And we should speak to Molly too – about where he was that night.'

Boase had just parked his car at the top of Killigrew and stepped onto the road, when a small car veered around the corner, nearly knocking him down. Boase saw the driver clearly. It was Edward James. In an instant, Boase was back in his own car and chasing after him. The two cars sped towards Penryn paying no heed to other traffic on the road. On and on they raced with Boase trying to keep up. James had the faster car and by the time Boase had reached Treluswell, the first vehicle had vanished. Determined to catch up, he continued on the Truro road. Reaching a bend in the road at Perranarworthal he saw James's car lying on its side in a ditch. He jumped out and ran across to the stricken vehicle. As he did so his quarry was walking away.

'James ... James ... stop.'

Edward James, shocked from his accident, turned and saw Boase. He sat down in the hedge.

'What are you playing at? You might have been killed driving like that. Why are you running away – you're not making it look good for yourself, are you?'

'I'm getting away from her. She's a nasty piece and I've had enough.'

'Molly?'

'Yes. Molly. I don't care if I never see her again.'

'Well, I'm sorry to say, you probably will see her again. You have to come back with me; we need to talk to you again. Come on, the car's just here.'

He led the man across the road to his car and they returned to Falmouth. As they walked into the police station, Boase addressed Constable Rabone.

'There's a car out at Perranarworthal in a ditch – bit of a mess. Get someone to arrange to have it moved, will you?'

Bartlett was sitting at his desk when Boase entered the room.

'James is downstairs, sir. He was driving away when I got to Killigrew. I chased him and, well, he crashed his car out at Perranarworthal.'

'Is he all right?'

'Bit shook up but he'll live.'

'Let's speak to him now – have him brought up.'

Bartlett and Boase sat with Edward James in their office. Bartlett leaned forwards on his chair.

'Why were you running away? You know you're a suspect in two murders, don't you?'

'I didn't do it. Your boss knows that – *and* his boss. That's why they let me go.'

'But someone has said they saw you heading towards Hunter's Path at the right time.'

'Who said that? They're lying, it's not true.'

'Well, someone is going to speak to your wife in a minute to find out what she knows about all of this.'

'Well, *she'll* stitch me up like a kipper – we can't stand each other. *That's* why I was leaving.'

'Nevertheless, we *will* be speaking to her.'

Boase cast a glance in Bartlett's direction. Was the older man thinking the same, he wondered. He listened as Bartlett continued.

'Were you clearing off because the money had run out – now that Clicker is gone?'

'Of course not. It was never *my* idea to take his money. Molly said that he owed her because he hadn't been around when she was a kid. I said that wasn't *his* fault – her mother had made the decision to leave when she was a baby.'

'So how can you explain why you were going to the seafront that night?'

'Well I can't, because I wasn't. That's the truth of it.'

'But we have a witness prepared to swear on oath that you were. We also examined your gun and it had one bullet missing which was the same type that killed Clicker.'

'It's nothing to do with me, I've told you.'

'Could someone have stolen it from you and then replaced it?'

'That must be what happened because *I* wasn't there, *I* didn't kill him.'

'What about Anne Warner?'

'To Hell with you, man! You saw for yourself– I was asleep when it happened. Just leave me alone. I've already complained about you lot once.'

Edward James was taken to back to his cell and Bartlett and Boase went to see Molly. As they arrived, she was outside the caravan grooming the ponies.

'Molly, you need to know that we're holding your husband on suspicion of your father's murder and possibly in connection with the murder of Anne.'

'What's it got to do with me?'

'We need to speak to you, Molly. Can we go inside?'

Molly sat in the small kitchen of the caravan and looked at Bartlett and Boase.

'Molly, did Edward leave here the night your father was killed?'

'Yes. He did. We were on early in the show. Afterwards he said I was not pulling my weight in the act. We had a huge row and he stormed out.'

'Did he take his gun?'

'I can't say – he had left before I came back.'

'What time did he return?'

'Oh, about two or three, I'm not really sure, I was quite sleepy but I heard the door and looked at the clock.'

'Had he said anything to you about your father that day?'

'No, I don't think so. Nothing.'

Bartlett and Boase left the recreation ground and returned to the station.

'What do you make of all this, Boase?'

'Not at all sure, sir. What do we know? Clicker was shot through the head. Edward James was seen near Hunter's Path. His gun had one bullet missing which was exactly the same as the bullet that killed Clicker. His wife says he went out after the show and didn't return until the early hours. Howard Smith has signed a statement to say he saw James that night. It's beginning not to look good for him.'

'That's what I think. Why would Smith say that if it wasn't true? Mind you, I don't see how he was anything to do with Anne – his clothes were perfectly clean when I saw him and he wasn't the least bit agitated.'

'That's as may be, but I've seen people in the war like that – just kill someone and calmly return to their duties.'

'Surely that's different though?'

'I don't think so – takes a certain type of person and there are people like that about. And isn't it suspicious that he was so calm – *and* clean?'

'You saying he's committed two murders?'

'No. But I'm keeping an open mind. If he only killed Clicker then we have another murderer at large and Greet's not going to like that.'

'No, you're right there.'

A knock at the door relieved the pair's concentration.

'Come in.'

The desk sergeant looked into the room.

'Thought you should know, sir, Superintendent Greet took a statement from a woman while you were out. Says she saw Edward James walking along beneath Hunter's Path that night. She was out walking her dog. She looked at him because he was only wearing a thin shirt and it was quite nippy that evening. Says it was definitely him.'

'Why is *he* taking statements?'

'Said because you weren't here, he didn't want anyone else doing it.'

'Is the woman absolutely sure?'

'Greet says it's a positive identification. Cuppa, sir?'

'I wouldn't say no. Thank you.'

Bartlett looked at Boase.

'This is even worse for him, isn't it, my boy?'

Chapter Eight

As the days turned into weeks, Greet became determined to tie up the murder case. Much to Bartlett's annoyance, the superintendent had taken matters very much into his own hands, although, thankfully, had seen fit not to bow to pressure from the London police to allow them to investigate. Greet had reassured the powers that be that the case was nearing an end and they'd accepted that.

'I don't think Edward James killed Clicker and Anne, sir. You don't either, do you?'

'No, I don't believe I do. Greet's nailed him for Clicker and I think as he's so sure of his evidence, we can't do anything about it. I hope to God he's right on this – he thinks he knows everything and we haven't got any better argument so that's that. But, no, I'm not satisfied with the Anne Warner business. Not a jot. Greet has that all wrong.'

'Well, if we really believe that, it means even with James awaiting his obvious fate there's still a killer lurking. We have to do *something*.'

'I think so. Greet is being so difficult about this. He's saying that he did all the work on the Clicker case, which is not in the least bit true, as you know, and we should have tied off the Anne case. I feel bad for her sisters. They won't rest until we find out what happened.'

'Let's revisit it, sir. Go back to the start. We can't leave it like this.'

'What do you mean? What can we do?'

'We need to look at this with a fresh pair of eyes.'

'At my time of life, my eyes are anything *but* fresh, Boase.'

'Yes, never mind that, sir. Go back to the beginning. The evening I saw Clicker – I was one of the last people to see him alive probably. And I saw Anne. Now, do you remember why she was talking to him?'

'About Margaret Field.'

'Yes. She was showing him that newspaper – we didn't fully deal with that, did we?'

'Why would that be relevant?'

'What if someone else had seen that paper?'

'I don't understand what you mean.'

'We didn't keep the newspaper– we gave it back to Anne. Do you remember?'

'Yes, yes, I do. Go on.'

'What if someone else saw the paper and knew she had told Clicker – that could be a reason to kill her. And there's only one person I know that could have a motive for that.'

The two men spoke together.

'Molly James!'

Bartlett leapt from his chair and grabbed his coat.

'My boy, I've been so damned stupid. We didn't entertain the fact that she could be the killer. Come on, we need to get up there now.'

The pair fetched a car and drove straight to Molly James' caravan. They got out and hammered on the door.

'Try round the other side, Boase. Look – the ponies are gone.'

Bartlett was looking through each window when he heard a shout behind him.

'Mr Bartlett ... Mr Bartlett!'

He turned to see Arthur Wayland, the lion tamer.

'You won't find Molly James, she's gone.'

'Gone where?'

'I'm not sure – she came over yesterday to speak to Pearl and me. She said that now Edward had been arrested for her father's murder, she had no need to stay.'

'Did she not give any idea of where she was going?'

'No. I didn't like to ask. She wanted to know if we'd look after the ponies. She said we could sell them if we wanted to but just to make sure they went to a good home. Is she in some sort of trouble, Mr Bartlett?'

'Nothing for you to worry about, Mr Wayland. And you have absolutely no idea where she might be?'

Arthur Wayland took off his cap and scratched his head.

'She hasn't been here as long as most of us and she didn't seem to fit in as well as the rest of us. I always thought it was because of her husband – terrified of him, she was. Good job you caught him, Mr Bartlett. But...'

'But what, Mr Wayland?'

'Well, she *did* say she had a friend who worked at the Picturedrome in Redruth. I think it was a local girl she'd met a few years ago when she was on holiday. She said she wanted to see her while she was in Falmouth because when we leave here she might never come back.'

'Do you know the name of this friend?'

'I'm sorry, I don't think she said.'

'Another thing, Mr Wayland – did you see or hear anything when Anne was attacked? Did you see anyone near the Warner caravan?'

'I'm just trying to think. Wait a minute. Pearl came out to the gate – she was waiting for a meat delivery, food for the lions. The delivery was late, so she walked up to the road – she thought the driver might be lost. She came back after about twenty minutes, she said she was a bit cold standing waiting and needed a cardigan. I said I'd go up and wait instead. I walked just over there – look.'

Wayland was pointing to a spot just opposite the Warner caravan and about twenty yards from it. Bartlett looked to where he was pointing.

'So you were quite close?'

'Yes.'

'Please think, sir. Did you see anyone?'

Wayland contorted his face and scratched his head. Boase sighed as the man closed his eyes.

'Wait a minute. Yes. Yes – I saw Molly James. She was wearing a headscarf and a raincoat. She was coming out of the Warner caravan.'

'Mr Wayland, this may be very important – are you absolutely sure?'

'Yes, I am, because Pearl saw her from the window. When I came back with the meat she was furious because she had just bought the exact same headscarf and said she wouldn't be able to wear it now that Molly had an identical one. Yes, that's it, that's who I saw. I came back, left the meat and that's when I saw you and Constable Boase come to the caravan.'

'You've been very helpful, thank you. Tell your wife we'll need to speak to her.'

Boase reappeared from the other side of the caravan.

'Mr Wayland here has just been telling me that Molly has left.'

Boase sat down on the step of the caravan and sighed, his shoulders slumped.

Wayland made to move.

'Sorry, Mr Bartlett – I need to be getting on if you don't mind.'

'You carry on, sir – and thank you.'

Boase stood up, dejected.

'This is all *my* fault – how did I let this happen?'

'We're in this together, Boase. No recriminations – we just need to work this through. Wayland said she had a friend in Redruth, someone who works at the Picturedrome. We should head on over there as soon as we can.'

Bartlett and Boase picked up two constables from the police station and made their way to Redruth to look for Molly James.

'You know this is a long shot, sir – she may not even be in the county.'

'Well, we have to hope our instinct is right this time. It's got to be her who killed Anne, just *has* to be – it all fits.'

The car drew up outside the Picturedrome which was closed. Bartlett peered through a window and saw a woman cleaning inside. He knocked on the glass and beckoned to her. She came over and opened the door.

'What? There's no pictures showin' 'ere till tonight. You'll 'ave to come back later.'

'Madam...'

As Bartlett spoke, the uniformed constables Eddy and Coad came alongside him.

'Oh ... you the police? Well, this is a respectable establishment – we don't want no trouble 'ere.'

'I would just like to speak to the proprietor, that's all. This is an urgent police matter.'

The woman held open the door and the four

112

men entered. They found themselves in a large hall.

'Wait 'ere.'

The woman disappeared.

Boase wandered around the hall looking at the posters advertising the latest films. He loved the cinema, *especially* going with Irene. Bartlett opened two or three doors leading off and quickly closed the last as the woman returned leading a tall, thin man. The man wore a silvery-grey suit which was too long in the arms and too short in the legs. Bartlett looked up at him as he approached.

'I am George Jago. May I help you?'

'Well, I hope you can, sir. I am investigating a murder...'

'Is that the Falmouth murder? Or murders, I heard there were two?'

'And what do you know about all this, sir, may I ask?'

'Well, nothing other than what I read in the paper – what a terrible business! And what has this to do with me – why are you here?'

'How many female staff do you have here at the moment?'

'I can assure you none of my staff would be involved in something like that. Absolutely not.'

'Please just answer the question – we're in a terrible hurry.'

'Oh. Let me see – well, there's Dolly Simmons – she's the cleaner you just met. Peggy Rowe, she helps with the films and screening and such like.'

'How old is Peggy?'

'I'd say fifty, maybe.'

'Go on. Who else?'

'Sarah Pollard. She runs the little refreshment kiosk.'

'Age?'

'She's quite young – I think about twenty-seven or eight.'

'Where does she live?'

'I'll have to check the staff records for that. Is she in trouble?'

'We don't think so but she may be able to help us. The address please?'

George Jago walked across to a small office and Boase watched him as he rummaged through an old desk. He drew out a large book.

'It'll be in here. Shall I write it down for you?'

'Yes please, sir.'

Boase took the sheet of paper with the girl's name and address and the police group left the Picturedrome.

'What's the name of the street, Boase?'

'Um, Plain-an-Gwarry.'

'Know where that is?'

'I'm a Redruth boy, sir.'

Arriving outside the house, Bartlett and Boase left the two constables standing by the car and went up the neat front path. Bartlett knocked at the door. Boase stepped back and looked up at the top windows. As he did so, the front door opened and a young woman stood there. Bartlett introduced himself.

'Excuse me, miss. We were wondering if you were an acquaintance of Molly James?'

'Molly? Yes, I am.' The girl looked flustered.

'Is she here, miss?'

'She's just left. She *was* here.'

'Where is she?'

'I don't know – why? What has she done?'

Bartlett ignored the question. Meanwhile Boase had gone around the back of the house. As he went up to the kitchen door, a window opened upstairs and a small valise was thrown down, narrowly missing Boase. He looked up to see Molly James about to climb out after it.

'Don't be silly, just come down. We want to speak to you.'

Soon, Bartlett and Boase were sitting in the parlour in Plain-an-Gwarry with Molly James.

Bartlett looked at the woman, who was now crying.

'Molly, tell us what happened with you and Anne Warner. We know you went to her caravan around the time she was killed; more than one person saw you.'

Molly cried again.

'She said Edward killed my father – she was telling everyone; and those two sisters of hers, they were saying it too.'

'Molly, *did* you kill Anne?'

'No. Of course I didn't.'

'We'll find out, Molly. Tell us what happened. Were you angry with her for blaming Edward?'

'Of course I was angry – but I didn't kill her. And what do you mean, you'll find out? You think you've found Edward out but you haven't. He's not a murderer.'

'But he's got a violent past, and you're frightened of him.'

'Yes, he's got a bit of a temper – but who hasn't?

115

It doesn't make us all murderers, does it?'

Molly wiped her eyes.

'You still need to find my father's murderer, Inspector. It wasn't Edward.'

Bartlett felt uncomfortable. Molly was saying just what he himself thought, that Edward James hadn't killed Clicker. But then *who* had?

'Molly, we're taking you back to Falmouth, to the police station. We've got a lot of questions we want to ask you and it's not an appropriate setting here. Get your things.'

Arriving back at the station, Molly James was taken to a cell to await questioning. Bartlett hung up his coat and Boase made some tea.

'This is getting worse, Boase. Molly is bound to stand by her husband, but I don't believe it of him either.'

'But Greet's taken it out of our hands and he's got cast-iron witnesses.'

'So he says.'

'Well, how can we go back now? The poor chap's run out of time and the noose is looming closer. It's a terrible business.'

'Well, we'll let Molly calm herself a bit before we speak to her. It looks bad for her, never mind Edward. What a nightmare this is turning into!'

Bartlett lit his pipe. Boase always thought it was funny that he always did so when he was thinking.

'Molly, tell us what happened when you went to Anne's caravan.'

'OK, I went to borrow some milk. Edward couldn't have any tea and he was going mad.

Anne invited me in and filled the jug. While I was waiting I saw the newspaper on the table. It had a story about my mother and that she had died seven years ago. I felt awkward but, not only that, I knew then that Anne must have told my father that my mother was dead. But I didn't kill her.'

'But that was the *first* time you went there. I'm talking about the day she died – you were seen leaving the caravan.'

'I wasn't there, I swear I wasn't.'

'We have more than one reliable witness, Molly.'

'I don't care. I didn't kill her.'

'Did you see anyone else when you were there?'

'No, because I wasn't there. Stop trying to trick me!'

'Did your husband know that Margaret Field was dead?'

'Yes. He said I shouldn't be asking my father for money all the time, but I needed it. Ed's a drinker and we never have enough money – my father could afford it.'

'No, he couldn't really – he always gave you his last.'

'I suppose the little fool, Anne Warner, told you that?'

'It doesn't matter who told me, it's a fact.'

'Look, I found out that Anne knew, that's all. I never even said anything to her. She must have told my father that my mother was dead – the silly old man probably killed himself.'

'What makes you say that, when you know he was shot through the head?'

'I don't know but it wasn't Ed – why would he

do such a thing?'

'Because Clicker was going to stop the money?'

'You're wrong, I tell you, you're wrong – Ed wasn't interested in the money.'

Bartlett and Boase left Molly in her cell and asked Penhaligon to take her some tea.

'Edward James wants to see me, Boase. Says he can explain more about Clicker.'

'Really?'

'Well, his trial *is* next week – the least I can do is to see what he has to say. You know how uneasy I am about all this.'

'You and me both, sir. But he's up at Bodmin. Do you want me to come with you?'

'No – he asked for me. I'll let you know what he says. How about you come over to us for supper this evening? Caroline said she'd like to see you again – and you know Irene would.'

'Thank you – that would be very nice.'

'Righto. I'm going to see James now. Lord only knows what this is about. I don't know what time I'll be back – oh, tell Greet you haven't seen me.'

Bartlett sat in the cell with Edward James. The man looked thin and pale and had an unkempt beard.

'Are they treating you all right?'

'Well, look at me.'

'What did you want to see me about?'

'They're going to hang me, Mr Bartlett. I know it.'

'You don't know that. Tell me what you want to say.'

'I didn't kill my father-in-law.'

118

'But what about the witness statements? At least one woman saw you. And your gun was damning evidence.'

'I did go there that evening after the show.'

Bartlett stood up and scratched his head.

'Why didn't you say so before? What were you doing there?'

'Clicker was upset – he said he knew me and Molly were swindling him out of his money – he'd found out somehow. I told him it wasn't me – that it was all Molly's idea and I'd been trying to stop her. I thought she was wrong.'

'So, what happened?'

'I saw him leave the recreation ground and head towards the seafront. I followed him. He was ever so shaken. I just wanted him to come back. I said we could sort it out – there was no point in getting upset.'

'I can see why he would be, Mr James. Did you have your gun?'

'No. No I didn't. I saw him go up the place they call Hunter's Path. I asked him to come back but he wouldn't – he told me to leave him alone. I went for a walk along the beach, then I came back and went to bed.'

'Well, my advice to you is to tell your solicitor what you've told me and to speak up at your trial.'

'No one will believe me, Mr Bartlett – you must see that. I just wanted you to know that I'm not long for this world. And that I didn't kill anyone.'

Edward James buried his head in his hands and sobbed.

Bartlett patted the man's shoulder.

119

'Please, Edward, you must tell them what you've told me. If this is all true there may be a chance for you. Please tell them.'

'Thanks for coming, Mr Bartlett. I really appreciate it. Maybe when I'm gone they'll catch whoever did this.'

Edward James offered out his hand to Bartlett who took it in both of his and shook it.

'Goodbye, Mr Bartlett.'

'Goodbye, Edward.'

'Tell Molly I love her.'

Boase sat in the parlour with Caroline and Irene. He looked at the clock. It was half past eight.

'I thought Dad would be home from Bodmin by now, Mum.'

'Yes, so did I, dear – he's obviously been delayed. He said he had something very important to deal with. I suppose he'll be back soon. Archie, would you like another piece of cake?'

'No, thank you. It was lovely, but I've had plenty.'

Boase couldn't feel hungry. Here he was with the love of his life – there was nowhere he'd rather be – yet he was uncomfortable. He was feeling for Bartlett; he knew the older man didn't really want to see Edward James but was a man of his word and always ready to help anyone if he could.

At half past nine, with still no sign of his boss, Boase left for home. He had offered to stay with Caroline and Irene but they wouldn't hear of it and, besides, they thought he looked tired. Boase took a walk along the seafront and turned over the recent events in his mind. *Who killed Clicker?*

Bartlett didn't think Greet was looking in the right direction and Boase himself didn't know what to think. *And what of Anne Warner?* That was a shocking business. *Did* Edward kill her – or was it really Molly? Yes, what a fine kettle of fish this was turning out to be.

Boase sat on the sand until about eleven o'clock then, suddenly realising he was tired and hungry, he walked back up to his room in Melvill Road.

Bartlett and Boase with Constables Eddy and Rabone returned to the recreation ground. Bartlett had tossed and turned all night, agonising over Molly James. She had a very good motive but without firm evidence, well, they could do nothing. The sun had broken through after a morning of rain as the four arrived. Bartlett gave his instructions, clearly.

'I'm certain there must be something here to incriminate that woman. The very crime scene is yards from where we are standing – she must have left a clue. You have to use your wits and everything you have in you to help me here.'

Constable Eddy spoke.

'But what if your hunch is wrong, sir? What if it's not her?'

'Well, yes, I could be wrong – but someone did it. And someone must have left some evidence, a clue to who they are. Right, do your best all. Please do your best. Eddy, you come with me. Rabone, you go with Boase. Remember I took the precaution of clearing this with the big cheese – search if you need to. Happy hunting.'

121

Two hours passed and the four met up again. Boase looked disgruntled.

'Sir, there's nothing here. We've spoken to people again, searched everywhere.'

Bartlett rummaged in his pocket for a match.

'Searched all the hedges around the ground?'

Rabone nodded.

'Yes, sir.'

'Bet you haven't looked in there.'

Bartlett indicated to the lion enclosure.

Rabone swallowed.

'No. No, sir, we haven't.'

'Well, neither have we, have we Eddy? Come on then.'

The four walked towards the lion enclosure, Rabone and Eddy lagging behind nervously. Bartlett turned and looked behind him.

'Come on you clots – you don't think you could go in there unsupervised do you? You should see your faces. I wouldn't let you just wander in there, would I?'

Now it was Boase's turn to look a little pale as they walked alongside a large pile of dung which looked like it had been left there for some time.

'Wonder what they do with that lot, Boase? Don't suppose they can easily dispose of it.'

'You should take some for your roses, sir.'

'That's an idea, Boase. Well done.'

'Sir, I was joking.'

'No – that's a sound idea, my boy. I don't know about roses but they say it's good to keep cats off the garden.'

'But you've got Topper for that, sir.'

Bartlett smiled and as Boase looked at him, the smile turned to an inquisitive frown.

'Upon my word. What's that?'

Bartlett stepped closer to the lion dung.

'Boase – what's that glinting?'

'Where, sir?'

Bartlett pointed with the end of his pipe to an object glimmering and largely concealed but for a fragment. 'Rabone, get in there and see what that is.'

Rabone looked incredulously at his superior.

'Me, sir?'

'Yes. You. Get a move on.'

Rabone looked over his shoulder at Eddy who was grinning from ear to ear.

'Well, you can stop or you'll be helping him.'

Bartlett was growing impatient.

As Rabone stepped onto the pile of manure, he lost his footing and fell on his front.

Boase laughed loudly.

'It's *not* funny, Boase.'

Bartlett's shoulders began to move as he tried to conceal his laughter.

'What is it, Rabone?'

'Sir, I think it's a knife wrapped in a handkerchief.'

Boase stepped forward.

'Don't touch the handle, Rabone.'

Rabone cautiously dug into the manure and lifted out the knife by its blade.

Bartlett puffed out his cheeks in relief.

'Good work. Boase, we need to get that sent to check for fingerprints. Let's hope that someone has left us some.'

Chapter Nine

Bartlett and Boase drank their tea in silence.

It was some weeks after they had first arrested Edward James, and that morning he had been hanged for the murder of Clicker the Clown.

After the find at the lion enclosure, statements had been taken from four people who said they had witnessed Molly James leaving the caravan around the time Anne Warner had been murdered and she was now waiting to stand trial.

Bartlett puffed on his pipe.

'I feel terrible about all this, Boase, and no error.'

'Don't you think she killed Anne? We have evidence now. The knife we found was used to kill Anne and it had Molly's prints on it.'

'Yes, I know. But I feel uncertain about Edward.'

'He had a fair trial, sir.'

'Greet was behind all this and I find him to be severely lacking.'

'You can't keep getting upset over it though, sir. The evidence was there, the witnesses added up.'

'Yes, but I keep thinking about what he told me the day I went up to Bodmin. He was trying to look out for Clicker – he was worried about the old man because he kept saying he was really upset about Margaret and Molly.'

'But, if *he* didn't kill him, who did? You've got

to believe it was him.'

'Have I?'

'What's the alternative?'

'I don't know, Boase. What about Molly?'

'But there's no evidence that says she killed her father. None.'

'What does that prove? People get away with murder, you know that.'

'You can't afford to think that was a mistake now, sir. It'll drive you mad.'

'I know, I know.'

'Look, sir, Edward James has gone – there was evidence against him. We can't change that.'

Boase pulled Bartlett's coat down from the coat stand and handed it to him.

'Are we going somewhere?'

'Yes. The "Seven Stars" – I'm buying you a pint.'

'But it's only eleven o'clock.'

'Come on – you need to get out of here.'

The two men took the short walk down to the Seven Stars on the Moor.

'Two pints of bitter please, Harry.'

Boase laid his coins on the bar and he and Bartlett sat at a table in the corner.

'What's this all about, Boase? Why are we here drinking beer at this hour?'

'We're here because of you – you needed to clear your head. You have to stop this way of thinking about Edward James. The law says he killed Clicker and, well, that's that.'

'I know that but it doesn't stop me from feeling uneasy about the whole business.'

'Who else could have done it? It was Edward's

gun. I really think, sir, that you're going to have to accept that he lied to you when you went to Bodmin.'

Bartlett and Boase finished their drinks and walked back to the police station.

'Cuppa, sir?'

'If you like.'

As Boase opened the door, Constable Penhaligon was standing outside and about to knock.

'Sorry to interrupt you – Mr Charles Trevarthen is here to see you both. Says he wants to talk to you about something important.'

Bartlett and Boase looked at each other and shrugged.

'Send him in, Penhaligon. Thank you.'

Charles Trevarthen entered the office.

'How do you do, Mr Trevarthen – how can we help you?'

'Well, I'm possibly too late but I wanted to tell you about my brother-in-law.'

Bartlett invited Charles Trevarthen to take a seat.

'How can that be of interest to us, sir?'

'My brother-in-law is Howard Smith.'

'Howard Smith from the circus?'

'Yes, that's the fellow. I've just heard that Edward James has been hanged. Is it true that Smith gave evidence against him?'

'Well, Smith *was* a key witness, yes. Why do you ask?'

'I am of the opinion that Smith had an axe to grind.'

'How come?'

'Well, I'm afraid it's rather a long story. My sister, Gertrude, married Smith in 1903. Their son Gregory was born a year later. Smith was a bad egg from the start and my parents didn't want Gertrude to have anything to do with him. Well, a couple of years after the wedding he was involved in a bank job – they were living in the Midlands. It was a huge sum of money, about thirty thousand pounds, I think. The gang would probably have got away with it if it wasn't for one person – Edward James. He was only a young man at the time – about seventeen, I'd say. Well, the gang was caught – all except Smith. Edward James had been across the street when the bank was raided and he recognised Smith. He came forward and gave evidence – upshot was that Smith got seven years.'

Boase leaned forward in his chair.

'So, how does this relate to the trial of Edward James?'

'Well, when Smith came out of jail he felt he'd lost everything. Gertrude had taken the baby to my parents – she was finding things difficult on her own. After about two years, she'd met another fellow and they moved into a place together with Gregory. So, you can imagine how Smith felt when he got out. He vowed he'd get even with James. I didn't even know that he was here until I took my family to the circus – just the sort of damned fool idea he'd have. Joining the circus, I ask you.'

Trevarthen sat back on his chair and tutted. Bartlett lit his pipe.

'And? What exactly are you trying to tell us, Mr Trevarthen?'

'I'm not sure, except to say that I find it all rather strange that he gave evidence against Edward James after openly admitting back then that he'd do anything, yes, anything to get even.'

Bartlett got up from his seat.

'But this is extraordinary! Are you actually telling us that Smith's statement might have been false, and made just to get back at Edward James?'

'I'm worried that may be the case.'

'But ... but, why on earth didn't you say something before now? A man's been hanged, for goodness' sake.'

'I've only just found out what happened – I've been working away and have been out of the county for several weeks. My wife told me what's been going on when I returned yesterday. I'm so sorry, Inspector Bartlett.'

'This is incredible, Mr Trevarthen – but I don't suppose you can be held to account for any of this. I can see it's not your fault. Thank you for letting us know.'

'Is there anything I can do, Inspector?'

'Well, no, I'm sorry to say there isn't. But thank you, Mr Trevarthen. Are you still in touch with your sister?'

'My sister died twelve years ago – I guess that's why Gregory went with his father into the circus. That man's always been a loser. Good day, Inspector Bartlett. Constable Boase.'

Bartlett sat back down in his chair.

'I knew it. I knew it. I had a feeling something wasn't right. Didn't I say to you, Boase?'

'But you couldn't know that Smith would give false evidence – or even that it was false evidence.'

128

'No, but I *knew* something was wrong – I should never have let Greet interfere.'

'You couldn't stop him, sir.'

'He thinks we take too long over things, Boase, but look what happened in his haste.'

'Well, there's nothing we can do now, sir, except hope that the evidence was truthful and valid. And really there was no one else it could have been – it was Edward's gun.'

'Yes, but did Greet find out if someone else could have taken it?'

'Well, we know he investigated every eventuality.'

'So *he* says. And...'

'And what, sir?'

Bartlett leaned back in his chair and looked out of the window onto the street below.

'What if there was another gun the same? Did he look into that?'

'Sir, I don't know– you're asking me impossible questions. What are the chances of there being another gun the same? *We* didn't look far into that, if we're honest.'

Boase had had enough. Bartlett was letting this prey on his mind now, and in a negative way.

'Sir, you really have to drop this now.'

'No, I don't. I'm going to see Howard Smith.'

'Sir, please. Just leave it!'

Bartlett was already putting on his coat and was out of the door by the time Boase had got up from his seat to follow.

Bartlett knocked at the door of Howard Smith's caravan. He waited and soon Gregory Smith answered.

'Young man, is your father in?'

'Yes. Come in. Dad, someone to see you.'

Howard Smith was reading a newspaper. He stood up.

'Gregory, go and get me some fags.'

The older man tossed a coin in his son's direction as he left the caravan.

'What do you want?'

'I have a reason to suspect you of being disingenuous.'

'What are you talking about?'

'The statement you gave about Edward James ... was it true?'

'Course it was true – everyone knows he killed the old man.'

'I'm not interested in your opinion – were you telling the truth when you said you saw Edward James going to the seafront?'

Howard Smith laughed.

'No. No, I didn't see him. But why wouldn't he kill the old man? He was happy to keep taking his money, everyone knew that. That man ruined my life – I even nearly lost my kid because of him ... and spent seven long years banged up ... yes, and it was all down to him.'

'Are you telling me that you gave a false statement and lied on oath at that man's trial?'

Realising the situation, Howard Smith tried to run to the door but Boase stood across it.

'Arrest him, Boase.'

As Boase stepped forward, Howard Smith lunged at him, pushing him back through the small caravan door. Boase landed on his back at the bottom of the caravan steps and Smith was gone. Bartlett came running out of the caravan.

'You OK, Boase?'

'Sorry, sir.'

Boase was standing up and the two men looked after Smith who was running at top speed along the side of the wall to the exit.

'Do you think he'll come back, sir?'

'Yes. His son is here – and so we will be. I can wait. Put someone up here to look out for him on his return.'

'Will do, sir. So, looks like it's true then – I thought Trevarthen was making it up. It sounded so far-fetched, about that bank job and all.'

'Looks like he was right, though. Smith won't get away with this. Look – here's the boy back.'

Gregory Smith had returned with the cigarettes. 'Where's my dad?'

Bartlett put his hand on the boy's shoulder.

'He's just gone off – he'll be back, don't you worry.'

'What did you say to him?'

'Nothing, son.'

'I'm not your son – go away.'

Gregory ran up the caravan steps and slammed the door shut behind him.

Boase brushed off his coat and he and Bartlett returned to the station.

'I want him brought in, Boase – he won't get away with this. How could anyone harbour such hate for another human being? Greet is going to hear about this too. I *knew* he should have stayed out of this.'

Boase put a cup of tea in front of Bartlett and

131

sat down behind his own desk. Opening the drawer, he pulled out a paper bag.

'Hungry, sir? Only I've got a small pasty here if you'd like a corner.'

'No. Thank you, Boase. I don't even think I can eat my dinner tonight. I feel sick. I don't know what Caroline will say – and Irene, especially as she puts so much effort into cooking me a dinner. No, I couldn't eat a thing, that's for sure.'

'You will when you see it, sir. Just wait. You'll sit at the table, Irene will bring you a bottle of Leonard's and then some dinner – what's it tonight? Bet it's a steak pie with loads of gravy. Or, how about a piece of haddock with those lovely potatoes Irene makes? Then there'll probably be a suet pudding – or, no, wait, an apple pie!'

'Boase – are you angling for an invitation to supper?'

'Of course not, sir. I'm just worried for you – it's not like you to turn down your dinner. I'm just trying to build up your appetite.'

'You're getting on my nerves, that's what. Come round at seven. There's always plenty and Irene will be happy to see you.'

'You don't have to invite me, sir, really you don't.'

'Just say yes, before I change my mind.'

'Well, then – yes. Thank you, sir.'

Bartlett started to feel a bit better; Boase was very capable of cheering someone up – although he bordered perilously on irritating at times.

'Dad, is it true that when you were in London, you ate jellied eels?'

Caroline Bartlett held her handkerchief up to her mouth.

'I know, Mum – it's disgusting. I told Archie and he didn't believe that people ate that.'

Bartlett put down his knife and fork.

'I don't know who told you that, Irene, but I can most definitely assure you that it is not true. Yes, it's a local delicacy in my part of the world but I cannot imagine why anyone would want to put that into their mouth.'

Irene was giggling.

'I'm sure you told me that you had it before, Dad.'

'I never did – and now, if you don't mind, I want to continue with my meat and potato pie – which is very good, by the way.'

Boase smiled, happy to see Bartlett eating and seemingly having got over his earlier upset. He bent down towards the floor and held out a piece of meat for Topper who was lying next to him. The dog took it gently then promptly went to Bartlett and placed his paw on his master's leg.

'Oh, I see – Boase has run out of food and so you come to me? Well, here you are – this is for being a very good boy.'

Bartlett offered the dog some more meat and patted his faithful friend's head.

Caroline cleared away the plates.

'I was wondering if you two had any more wedding plans or news for us?'

'Oh, Mum, no – we haven't really had much time lately to talk about it, what with Archie being so busy at work.'

'Well, you need to talk about the church and of

course, the dress – and obviously a date. You must have a date in mind?'

'We were thinking about next Easter maybe – weren't we, Archie?'

'Yes, yes, that's right – and if that would be OK with both of you?'

Bartlett snorted.

'Of course it is. My word, it's not us getting married – you do whatever you like, we'll just string along. Isn't that right, Princess?'

'Of course it is, dear. I don't think you were very happy about our wedding arrangements, were you?'

'Only because your mother and her sister took over the entire proceedings and you didn't get what you really wanted.'

Caroline kissed her husband's head.

'But George, dear, I got exactly what I wanted.'

Bartlett looked uncomfortable. 'Stop being silly – and in front of these two.'

Boase and Irene laughed and Topper, letting out a sigh, went and lay on the mat.

By the next evening, it was apparent that Howard Smith had not returned to his caravan – and to his son. Bartlett had made it plain to Greet in no uncertain terms that this had been one enormous mess and that maybe an innocent man had been hanged because of shoddy and hasty investigations. Surprisingly, Greet offered no counter-attack.

'I told you, Boase – he just doesn't care. I sometimes don't even think he's human. He just stood there like a tailor's dummy. Never said a word.

He knows he's messed up on this. Now, that Smith – I want him. He's guilty of killing that man as surely as if he'd pulled the lever himself.'

'That's a bit strong, sir.'

'No it isn't, Boase. You can't have people going around accusing and giving false statements and evidence – especially in a serious case like this. You need to look at every tiny thing – you need to be accurate. *You* understand that, my boy – I know how disciplined and picky you are. That's what makes you so good at what you do. A policeman has to look at everything and not make hasty and impulsive decisions – Greet's failed in elementary skills here and, mark me, this is going to stick to him like glue.'

Boase was taken aback. He didn't ever remember Bartlett actually saying that to him before.

'But why didn't Superintendent Greet make sure he *was* accurate, sir?'

'My guess is that I've been right about him all along – he's a fake. He's been propelled up through the ranks simply because it was his turn – not because he was any good. Well, look at the trouble he's caused now – and how do we know he hasn't done this before?'

'Well, what can we do now, sir? I mean, to put things right?'

'Well, we can't raise the dead, Boase, but we can sure as hell catch that man and make him pay for what he's done.'

'But there was *other* evidence, sir – against Edward James.'

'Yes, I know, but that doesn't make that man's actions all right. He was the first "witness" and

135

now we know he couldn't wait to stitch up Edward James – simply as revenge. It's unbelievable. If Greet hadn't intervened, I know we would have had a different outcome. Greet took the lead from Smith's statement and made everything else fit around it. I'm sure of it. And, by keeping us at bay, we weren't able to stop him. This is a bad business, Boase, a very bad business. This isn't what policing is about – this isn't how it's supposed to work.'

'But if James didn't kill Clicker, who did?'

'That's what we need to find out, Boase – and we will. We will.'

Chapter Ten

Again, Boase couldn't sleep. He had so much on his mind. Irene, the wedding, Bartlett. Yes, Bartlett. Boase didn't like to see him so upset. As Boase lay on his pillow turning over the recent events in his head, he thought he heard a shout from below his window. Was that someone calling his name? *Surely not?* He listened again.

'Boase. Boase!'

Glancing at the clock, he threw back the covers and ran to the window. Opening it he looked down into the garden.

'That you, sir? It's half past one!'

'I know – you need to get dressed and come down!'

Boase hurriedly threw on his clothes and, moving quietly, went across the landing, down the stairs and out through the front door. Bartlett was waiting at the gate.

'What's going on, sir?'

'I left messages with everyone about Howard Smith – that they must let me know if he appeared. Well, Coad just came round to my house, as I asked him, I did say day or night – I guessed Smith'd appear at some ridiculous hour, under cover.'

'Was he at the caravan?'

'No. Coad and Rabone were patrolling about an hour ago when they saw him. They recognised him from when we were at the recreation ground before.'

'So where was he – and where is he now?'

'They said they saw him at Greenbank – come on, we're going there now. I walked here but I sent Coad back for a car – he's left Rabone waiting near Smith to make sure he stays put.'

'What? Smith will see him for sure – especially Rabone.'

'But they didn't expect to see him there.'

'Well, you told them to be alert – they should have been prepared.'

'It was Rabone who found him – then Coad just happened to be coming along and he sent him to fetch me. They did the right thing; there didn't seem to be any urgency – apparently he's holed up in that little nightwatchman's shed by the Greenbank Laundry – you know the one. Rabone saw him come out for a smoke, sitting on the wall, bold as you please. In this moonlight he was easy to spot. They couldn't have taken him in on their own without a car – look at the size of him. Here we are, here's the car.'

The car was driven swiftly from Melvill Road and towards Greenbank, arriving a few minutes later. Bartlett and Boase got out and walked towards Constable Rabone, who was standing by the wall and looking down on the laundry.

'Is he still here?'

'Yes, sir. He's inside that little shed. Look – down by the side of the laundry.'

'Yes, I know it. Right, Boase, you and Coad go down on this side, I'll go on the other. Rabone, you wait here in case he gets away. He can only come up past you – unless he jumps into the sea!'

The men took their places. The moon disappeared behind a cloud and the bay was lit only by a few twinkling lights from ships. Boase and Coad moved quietly along the side of the Greenbank Sanitary Laundry and found themselves at the back of the shed. Bartlett had appeared at the side. They could hear some noise from inside. As the moon reappeared, the three men waited silently for their opportunity. Bartlett could clearly see Boase and Coad now, and beckoned them to come around to the front of the hut. Coad, being in front of Boase, stepped forward and as he did so his heavy boot kicked an abandoned beer bottle. He grimaced and stood still as the bottle rolled down the small slope rattling as it went. Boase sighed. Suddenly, the door of the hut opened and Smith was standing in the doorway. From his position near the sea wall, Bartlett could clearly see the man, lit up by the dim oil lamp inside. Bartlett moved forward.

'Stay just where you are, Smith. It's the police.'

Boase and Coad ran forward towards Bartlett just as Howard Smith darted across to the sea wall, moving swiftly through the ten-foot gap between the three men. Bartlett spun round in time to see Smith jumping over the wall. The three men looked over the side. The moon had disappeared behind the clouds again and the sea was black. Boase listened. He could clearly hear the sound of the man in the water. He pulled off his overcoat and jumped up onto the wall. Bartlett grabbed him.

'Don't, Boase – let him go. He'll either come back or drown.'

Boase looked at Bartlett aghast. He knew Bartlett thought it unspeakable what Smith had done to help Edward James to the gallows but he was very surprised to hear him talk like this.

Boase continued looking into the sea for another fifteen minutes before Bartlett persuaded him to leave.

'Come on, Boase. There's nothing we can do but wait and see. Let's go home.'

Boase still felt uncomfortable with Bartlett's attitude but he took the older man's advice and went back to his lodgings.

Boase had seen little point in going back to bed when he reached home at a quarter past five in the morning, so made himself some porridge and washed before going to the station. Bartlett had done much the same thing and was already in their office, a cup of tea on his desk, when Boase arrived.

'Get any sleep, Boase?'

'No, sir. You?'

'No, I didn't bother. Greet's already been on at me – am getting sick of him, I am, straight. This is all *his* fault – I told him he shouldn't have interfered. Anyway, he knows the lot now. I told him about last night too.'

'What did he say, sir?'

'Well, he just tried to lay the blame at my door. He's well and truly crooked, Boase. I tell you he's crooked.'

Bartlett looked out of the window onto the street.

'Any news on Molly James, sir?'

'Oh, yes – had that out with Greet too. She's going before the magistrates on Monday.'

'That soon?'

'Well, I suppose there's no point waiting about – she's guilty, we all know that. But she didn't kill Clicker and neither did her husband.'

'What do we do now, sir? About all this business? We can't leave a murderer to get away.'

'You're telling me. But what do we do? Who else could have killed the old man? We've been through the whole circus troupe, we've got no other suspects outside. It doesn't make sense, Boase. Edward James had the gun that killed Clicker but it wasn't him that pulled the trigger. We know that now. Unless...'

'Unless what?'

'Well, we're saying that Edward's gun was the weapon. What if there was another identical gun?'

'It's not impossible, sir, but that type of gun isn't very common.'

'But, as you say, not impossible.'

140

'So what do we do? Ask everyone around if they own a weapon like that?'

'You know that's not what I'm saying, Boase, don't be awkward. We don't know that the killer is local anyway. But I'm not prepared to finish this here, no I am not. I am of the opinion that an innocent man has been put to death, the man who played the major part in that act has escaped us and Greet won't have any more to do with it. What a kettle of fish this is.'

Bartlett drank his tea and continued to look out of the window. He turned round as there was a knock at the door. Penhaligon stuck his head round it.

'Sorry to interrupt, sir. There's a young fellow here – Gregory Smith.'

'Gregory? Send him in, Penhaligon.'

Gregory Smith had been crying.

'Where's my dad?'

'I'm sorry, Gregory – we don't know where he is at the moment. We'd like to know where he is, too.'

'He's run away because of you. Why did you have to bully him like this? He hasn't done anything wrong. He hasn't killed anyone.'

'Look, I can't discuss this with you and I'm hoping your father will return home. Maybe you could let us know if he comes back?'

'What? You're kidding. You'd be the last to know. You've caused enough trouble.'

Gregory flung open the door, which banged against the hat stand behind, and went into the lobby. Boase followed him.

'Gregory, could I ask you a question?'

141

'What?'

'Your father – can he swim?'

'What has that got to do with anything?'

'I just wanted to know, that's all.'

'Funny sort of question – but no, he can't swim a stroke. In fact, he's terrified of the water.'

Gregory left through the main door and Boase returned to his desk. He looked at Bartlett.

'Did you hear that, sir?'

'Yes, Boase. I heard.'

Three days passed. Bartlett and Boase kept up each day with the details of the trial of Molly James and both had to give evidence. Howard James had not reappeared.

'Do you think he drowned, sir? He can't swim after all.'

'I don't know what's happened – it's public now, people have been out searching for him and unless he's been washed out to sea, I don't know what's happened to him. Greet's going mad up there but what more can I do? I didn't expect he'd do a foolish thing like that. Look here – it's all over the *Packet*.'

Boase picked up the *Falmouth Packet* and scanned the front page. News had got out somehow that the police were responsible for the disappearance of Howard Smith.

'I don't know, Boase. This is going from bad to worse: Edward James, hanged; Howard Smith, missing possibly drowned; and Molly James – when's the verdict?'

'I think tomorrow, sir.'

'Well, I'd have liked to go up there but I can't

get away. There was talk that she might get a jail sentence for what she did but I can't see that happening, can you?'

'No, sir, I can't. They found enough evidence against her apparently – the trial's been in all the papers. She's in it up to her neck, I'd say, sir, no joke meant. I don't like the death penalty any more than you do, but things aren't looking good for her – they said they found evidence of her being in the caravan at the time too.'

'Yes, well, I know deep down it was her – but she's such a young woman.'

'So was Anne.'

'I know, I know. You don't really think Molly would kill the old man, though, do you?'

'We now know she's capable of murder – but her own father?'

'Looks like they didn't have a very good relationship.'

'Yes, but it's too late now, sir. Edward James is gone and we have to get past that now.'

'You're right, but I'm not happy, Boase.'

Boase left that particular conversation there.

'Irene and her mother want to go for a picnic on Sunday – fancy it? I can't say I'm that bothered, I'd rather stay at home with a beer and the newspaper. But if I stay in, Greet might send someone round for me to come in and I don't really see what I can do at the moment.'

'Picnic it is then, sir. Thank you.'

Sunday came as a blustery day but that didn't deter the small group, including Topper, who made their way across the cliff path to Maenporth armed with plenty of food, a flask of tea and a good supply of Leonard's London Beer. Caroline Bartlett paused as the small beach came into view.

'You all right, Princess?'

George Bartlett offered his arm to his wife.

'I'm fine thank you, George. Just need a minute.'

'Irene, you two go on and find a nice spot, we'll catch you up. I'm sorry, Princess, this was a bad idea. It was too far for you to walk.'

'No. No, it wasn't. It's a lovely walk. I'm fine, really. Don't fuss now, dear.'

The four sat and ate, drank and talked and Topper ran in and out of the sea.

'Shall we have a little walk, Archie?'

'If you like – look, the tide's out quite a long way – we could walk round to the caves on the other side.'

Caroline put down her cup.

'Oh, do be careful, Archie – the tide can come in quite quickly here.'

'We won't be long, I promise.'

The two walked across the beach, hand in hand.

'You shouldn't worry about those two, Princess. That boy is more than capable of taking care of her – he'd never let anything happen to our girl.'

'I know, George, but she's still my baby.'

Bartlett smiled and pushed back a wisp of hair that had strayed across his wife's face.

'She's *my* baby too and I'm more than happy that she's safe with that young man. Now, any more of those ham sandwiches? The sea air always makes me hungry.'

Boase and Irene had strolled across to the other side of the beach and towards the caves. As Irene balanced on a rock, a wave came up and splashed over her. She shrieked.

'Oh, no! Archie, my shoes will be ruined. I should have listened to you and carried them. And my stockings are soaked. Do you mind if I just go around behind that rock and take them off?'

'Go on, Irene – I don't want you to catch a cold. Be careful, it's a bit slippery. I'll wait here.'

Irene disappeared around the rock and Boase waited, observing a nest up in the cliff. He watched to see if any birds would appear, half thinking he would have liked to have brought his paints. He turned and looked back across the beach. He could see Bartlett and Caroline, and a couple of other people walking their dogs. He watched as Topper continued to fetch sticks and seaweed from the shoreline. This was a far cry from the pressures of work and murder and trials and executions. As he stood and waited, a scream came from behind the rock. Boase ran like a whippet, leaping over rocks until he reached a small cave.

'Irene? IRENE!'

Irene was nowhere to be seen.

'Irene, answer me. Where are you? Irene?'

Boase entered the cave and walked further into the gloom. He could see a cigarette glowing in the darkness.

'Irene? Are you in here?'

Boase's heart was pounding now.

As he peered further into the blackness, he saw

145

Irene's face. She was being held, a hand over her mouth. As she was pushed towards him, Boase clearly saw Howard Smith behind her.

'Let her go, Smith. Let her go or I swear I'll kill you with my bare hands. Let her go.'

'Why should I?'

Boase could see, even in the dim light, that Irene was shaking.

'Let her go.'

'Only if you let *me* go.'

'OK. What do you want me to do?'

'I want you to give me a free pass back to see my boy and then to get of this town. I'm not going to be sent to prison again – I didn't do anything wrong, you know that. Edward James was a sneak and I paid him back. He got what he deserved.'

'You made up evidence and lied in court.'

'Well, if you want this girl back safely then you're going to have to overlook that.'

'Right.'

'How do I know I can trust you? You need to tell that boss of yours that he's not to touch me.'

'I'll tell him.'

Boase wasn't going to do anything to compromise Irene's safety – he'd worry about the consequences of his actions later.

'You make sure and tell him now.'

'I've said I agree, now let her go.'

Smith thrust Irene forward and she ran to Boase, sobbing. He held her to him and as he looked up again, Smith had gone.

'Archie, I want to go home. Please take me home.'

'It's all right, Irene, you're safe now.'

'Who was that horrible man?'

'You don't need to know about him – come on, let's get back to the beach.'

Taking her by the hand, Boase led Irene back across the rocks and onto the beach. As Irene saw her father, she ran to him and sobbed again. Bartlett looked up as Boase approached.

'Boase? What on earth has happened?'

As Caroline dried Irene's eyes, Boase told Bartlett about the encounter in the cave.

'I thought he'd drowned. How did he make it to here if he can't swim?'

'I have absolutely no idea, sir.'

Boase told Bartlett about the agreement he had just made.

'Well, you couldn't do anything else, could you? But I'm going to get him. Don't you worry about that. I'll get him.'

'Sir, I promised.'

'Well, *I* didn't.'

The picnic was quickly packed away and they all headed for home.

Chapter Eleven

'You're not *really* going to go after Smith are you, sir?'

'Well, as a matter of fact I am, Boase. Now I've got an even bigger axe to grind.'

'But I promised him he could go.'

147

'Well, I can see, at that moment, you might say that – and I'm glad you did, but when I think of him attacking Irene like that...'

'I know, sir. I had no choice but to agree, to keep Irene safe. I thought it was the right thing to do – I couldn't overpower him when Irene was there, and at risk.'

'Boase, just leave it to me – *I* didn't promise him anything and as far as I can see, you only promised that you'd try to keep me away from him. Well, you've tried. Your involvement in this particular event has ended.'

Bartlett went out into the lobby and slammed the door behind him. Boase didn't want to fall out with him and he knew Bartlett was right. He resolved there and then to put his promise to the back of his mind and to concentrate on the case, and on Irene.

Bartlett returned after five minutes and sat back down in his chair.

'I've just been up to see Greet. The verdict is back.'

Boase put down his ham sandwich and looked at Bartlett enquiringly.

'Guilty – no plea for mercy.'

'Can't they review it, sir?'

'No they can't. Really, why should they? She's guilty of murdering that young girl, I know it, you know it. Maybe we never fully understood the motive but she did it. Why would they show her mercy?'

'Do you think she killed her father, sir?'

'I don't know what to think – if she did, then

she's a double murderer and, worse, Edward James has been executed for nothing.'

'But we can't afford to think like that, can we?'

'No, my boy. No we can't. But it's an interesting idea.'

'What do you mean?'

'That she killed her father because the money had dried up and then pinned it on her husband. She would probably know where he kept the gun.'

'Is that all likely, sir?'

'At my age I'm beginning to think anything is likely, Boase. When I think about what I've seen over the years in this job, I think I can believe almost anything. Now, I wonder...'

'Wonder what, sir?'

'Well, if it *was* her who killed the old man, whether she tipped off Smith to give evidence against Edward. I've still got bad feelings about this and I think Greet was too hasty. It was all a bit too easy and too convenient, don't you think, Boase?'

'Why do you say that, sir?'

'I don't know, I'm just rambling now. I just wonder if they had some involvement in this whole thing together.'

'I think that's a bit far-fetched, sir. Smith confessed his reasons for what he did to Edward James.'

'Yes, he did – and that's why I'm going to get him and make him pay. Talking of that, have Coad and Eddy seen him turn up at the caravan yet?'

'No, we would have heard. They're taking it in

turns with Rabone. Nothing so far. He won't go in daylight hours, will he?'

'Not if he's got any sense at all. Did he say to you what his plans were?'

'No, just that he wanted to get out of Falmouth – and to be left alone to do it.'

'Well, that's not going to happen. We'll be ready for him when he comes.'

Boase finished his sandwich and went in search of more tea.

Heavy rain was lashing down as darkness fell. Arthur Wayland couldn't sleep. He sat up in bed and looked at the little clock on the table. Half past two. He leaned across to his wife and tapped her shoulder.

'Pearl. Pearl!'

'Oh, what is it? What do you want?'

'Can you hear that rain?'

'Well, yes I can, now you've woken me up. What time is it?'

'It's half past two. Do you want a cup of tea?'

'No. I just want to go back to sleep.'

'Be a good girl, make me a cuppa, will you?'

'Bleeding cheek – why should I make it when you just offered?'

'Because I just heard thunder. I'm going to check on the cats – you know they get agitated during a storm. I won't be long. Come on now, be a good girl, get up. Put the kettle on.'

'You shouldn't be going out in the middle of the night. You know Inspector Bartlett said that lunatic Smith might come back at any time and that we were to be on the lookout.'

'Yes, dear, I know but he's not likely to come out in this downpour, is he?'

'I don't know, I'm sure. If he really is a mad-man, who's to say what he might or might not do?'

'Yeah, well, if I see him, he'll get a piece of my mind – what a filthy trick. Inspector Bartlett told me all about it. I really liked that young man Ed-ward. Fair enough, he could get a bit nasty – bit like me in my younger days...'

'What d'you mean "in your *younger* days"?'

'You know I'm not like that any more, Pearl. Anyway, I was just saying, that was a damned vindictive thing to do – such a terrible business. Revenge and hate are awful things.'

Arthur Wayland pulled on his dressing gown and a pair of boots and went out of the caravan. The rain was falling even heavier now and lightning had just lit the sky. Arthur walked across to the compound. He could hear the lions pacing. He didn't like them to be upset; they were like friends to him. He unlocked the first door and entered, securing it behind him before he opened the second. He definitely didn't want any escapees. The four lions recognised their master and came over to the bars.

'It's all right. Come on now, calm down. It'll all be over in a minute. Here you are – here's a little treat.'

Arthur threw some morsels into the cage and continued to speak reassuringly – the lions seemed more settled now. Arthur, satisfied with this, retraced his steps to the first door. As he fumbled for the key, he looked through the small window which gave light into the compound. As the lightning flashed, Arthur clearly saw the figure of Howard Smith lit up in the momentary brightness. Unlocking both doors, Arthur ran outside shouting.

'Smith! Howard Smith!'

Smith saw Arthur and, rather than running away as one might expect, he ran towards the compound.

'You've got a nerve coming back here, Smith. After what you did to Edward James. You know the police are looking for you?'

'No, you're wrong, old man – I can come and go as I please.'

'The place is crawling with them – you'll never get away.'

'That's just where you're wrong.'

Smith stepped further towards Arthur Wayland and was now within a couple of feet of him. Arthur stepped back and as he did so, he heard a shout.

'Stop! Police! Stop and get down on the ground.'

Arthur could see Constables Eddy and Rabone running towards them. Howard Smith turned and as he too saw them, spun back around and, drawing a knife from his pocket, grabbed Arthur Wayland around his neck. Now behind the man, Smith was retreating towards the compound.

'Stand back or the old man will get hurt. Stand away!'

The two policemen advanced. Smith's grip on Arthur grew tighter.

'Right, open this door. Quickly!'

Arthur fumbled for the key and opened the

door. Smith dragged him inside. Arthur gasped almost silently as he realised that, in his haste to challenge Smith moments earlier, he hadn't shut the inner door. In over thirty years he had never left a door unlocked. As Smith continued to drag the lion tamer further inside, the two policemen pulled open the first door. Smith had his back to the inner door of the cage and the lions drew near. Arthur Wayland shouted out.

'Please. Let me go!'

All at once the biggest and oldest lion, hearing Wayland shout for his release, pounced upon Smith's back, ripping into his shoulders. The man was dragged back into the cage and as Arthur realised he was free, he turned towards the lions. He quickly shut his eyes but not before he had seen the remaining lions descend upon Howard Smith. As the two policemen moved forward, Smith's body was already lifeless on the floor.

Constable Eddy addressed Arthur.

'Quickly, shut that gate, sir. We can't help him now but we can save ourselves.'

Arthur obeyed and, locking the door, slumped to the floor, his head in his hands.

'They've never hurt anyone. They're not like that. They've never hurt anyone.'

'Greet wants to see me, Boase – about Smith. What can I tell him? That he got what he deserved last night? That he was a nasty piece of work?'

'I don't know, sir. I just don't know.'

'Well, I've got to go up at nine. I'm just stepping outside for a smoke and a think.'

'Righto, sir.'

Boase returned to some papers on his desk but he couldn't concentrate. Something just didn't add up in all of this. He drew a notepad from his drawer and made some notes:

1. *Clicker killed*
2. *Anne Warner killed*
3. *Edward James hanged*
4. *Molly James to be hanged*
5. *One gun impounded*
6. *Howard Smith mauled and killed by lions*

He re-read his list. No wonder Greet was furious. This didn't look good at all. As he closed the notepad, Bartlett returned.

'Right, I'm going up – I expect you'll hear him shouting from here. Anything you want me to ask?'

'Don't think so, sir. He's got to know that Smith had that coming last night – I think he was quite happy to make good his escape even if it meant killing Arthur Wayland.'

'Quite. You couldn't check up on his boy, could you? Maybe send someone round to see him – he must have an aunt or someone to help out. Or, what about the Trevarthens? I almost forgot them – he's their nephew. Sort something out, will you, Boase?'

'Of course I will – don't worry about that. Good luck!'

Bartlett had been right about the shouting. Boase could hear raised voices above his head and footsteps pacing the floor of Greet's office. He was worried that all this was getting too much for Bartlett. He made a pot of tea in preparation for the older man's return.

'I told him straight, Boase. I told him he was too hasty – he just carried on blaming me. He even had the blasted cheek to imply that I'm past it and maybe I should be thinking about retiring. He's been trying to get rid of me for a long time now. Well, he's not going to get the better of me.'

'So, what now, sir?'

'Well, he says we have to think about letting the circus move out now, that's it's a bad image for them and for the town. I can't say I disagree with that. We'll need to go up and see Chester Martin – let him know they can go soon.'

'Well, I won't be sorry to see the back of them, if I'm honest.'

'Me neither, Boase. Me neither.'

'And it's about time too. Have you got any idea how much money I've lost hanging around this godforsaken place? How many shows I've had to cancel around the country? How many people I've let down?'

'Well, none of that is my fault, Mr Martin – I've merely come to tell you that now you're all free to leave. Has Clicker's caravan been emptied?'

'Yes – why?'

'What happened to his personal effects?'

'There wasn't much there. Mostly junk. Why – has he got any other relatives?'

'I'm afraid to say not for much longer. Unless there's anyone besides Molly that you know of?'

'No. The old man didn't have a lot to say. Kept himself to himself really. What actually happened, Mr Bartlett? Do you even know?'

'Only what we've already stated. That, as far as we know, and in accordance with evidence given in a court of law, Edward James murdered his father-in-law, Molly James killed Anne Warner and Howard Smith was mauled to death by lions.'

'That was a bad business – I've never had any trouble with lions in my show – never. I don't believe it was Wayland's fault neither. Mind you, he should have been more careful over the double doors. Will there be an inquiry into that?'

'Well, yes, there will have to be, but I don't think that will affect you or your business – just the Waylands.'

'What about the boy? I can't take him with me now – he says he doesn't want to stay anyway.'

'Don't worry – we've been in touch with his uncle; he's going to take care of him for the time being.'

'Thanks.'

Bartlett shook the ringmaster's hand. He took his pipe from his pocket and turned to leave. Boase looked at Chester Martin.

'Can I ask you a question, sir?'

'If you like.'

'How long did you know Clicker?'

'Oh, for many years.'

'Since he was with Margaret Field?'

'Yes. I even tried to warn them about their carryings on. I told them no good would come of it. Clicker was heartbroken when she left. Yes, we went back a long way – we were the only two left from the old brigade.'

156

Boase sat back down on a chair. Bartlett looked at him and wondered what was on his mind.

'So, if he was a clown and you a ringmaster – well, how did you get together? Were you always in this circus?'

'Actually, no.'

Chester Martin began to look thoughtful.

'We were in another circus in Paris when we were young. We were very good friends – that was long before Clicker met Margaret. We were a team together – in fact, we were lion tamers.'

'Lion tamers?'

Bartlett came back and looked at Chester Martin.

'You never told us that before.'

'Why would I – it's practically ancient history.'

'Did you have guns?'

'Yes ... but ... now, look here, Mr Bartlett. I don't like what you're implying. I hope you don't think I killed the old man just because I owned a gun years ago.'

'I didn't say that, did I?'

'Well, I haven't got a gun now. In fact, we sold the act to Arthur and Pearl Wayland. Clicker felt he was getting too old and it was too risky – I think he just didn't want the worry of it all any longer. Arthur has a way with lions, always has had. And, no, before you even ask – *he* doesn't have a gun. He treats those lions like pet kittens and they're completely docile with him too.'

'Just not with anyone else. Right, thanks, Mr Martin – let me know when you're ready to leave the town. I'm guessing it'll take a day or two for you to get everything ready?'

157

'Yes, probably.'

'Right, cheerio then.'

Bartlett and Boase left the ringmaster and walked back down to the police station.

Chapter Twelve

At midday on Sunday, Archibald Boase was knocking on the Bartletts' front door. He had been invited by Irene for lunch. He waited on the step as Topper barked inside. Irene came running through the hall and, grabbing Topper's collar, pulled open the door.

'Hello, Archie, I've been looking forward to seeing you – come in.'

Boase wiped his feet on the mat and patted Topper. He kissed Irene's cheek. Caroline Bartlett came out of the kitchen wiping her hands on her apron.

'Hello, Archie. What beautiful blooms.'

Boase handed Caroline the bunch of flowers he had been carrying.

'Yes, they're for you – thanks for inviting me.'

'Well, I didn't – Irene did, but I'll take the flowers anyway.'

Caroline smiled as she looked at the bright yellow flowers.

'I love dahlias – look, Irene, they're just like a big bunch of sunshine.'

'They're lovely, Mum. Dad's in the parlour, Archie – go in, I'm just helping Mum.'

Bartlett was sitting in his armchair smoking his pipe. He looked round as Boase knocked on the open door and walked into the room.

'Good afternoon, sir.'

'Hello, my boy – how are you?'

'I'm fine thanks.'

'Drink?'

'That'd be lovely – I'm parched.'

Boase sat in the other armchair and sipped a pint of Leonard's.

'I don't want to talk shop with the girls around, Boase, but just before they come in, what were you thinking about Martin and Clicker being lion tamers?'

'Well, I don't know that I was thinking anything really – but it *is* strange, all this gun business. I mean, they're all packing up and leaving now but I still don't feel right about the whole thing.'

'So, say what's on your mind.'

'I'm not sure – but I'm beginning to wonder just how many guns there are around. We know lion tamers always keep one...'

'But we don't, do we? Martin says Arthur Wayland doesn't feel the need for one – mind you, he must be mad.'

'And unusual – I don't imagine many tamers *wouldn't* have a gun for protection.'

'Quite, but that wouldn't have helped Smith by all accounts, because he had a firm grip on Wayland and his back to the lions – what a fool. I agree, it's all a puzzle – especially now you're doubting the number of guns around.'

'Well, I'm probably wrong. I just don't know what is the truth of the matter. I suppose if you look at the whole thing from the outside, it's all over – Edward James dead, Molly almost so, and Smith – when you look at it like that, well, it's not much of a puzzle at all really, is it?'

'But, I don't think you're satisfied, are you?'

'No.'

'Nor me – and I think Greet has a lot of questions to answer.'

'But that'll never happen – he's so watertight he's practically squeaking.'

'But I can't let this go.'

'Is this *just* about getting back at Greet, or do you really doubt the outcome of this?'

Bartlett tapped his pipe on the fender.

'If I'm being honest? Bit of both probably. Seriously though, like you, I can't put my finger on it...'

At that, Caroline and Irene called from the dining room that food was ready and Bartlett, Boase, and Topper trooped to the table. Boase sat in his usual place next to Irene.

'This looks lovely, Mrs Bartlett – sorry, I mean Caroline. I keep forgetting.'

Irene laughed and Boase looked at her, thinking again how beautiful she was.

Caroline took a dinner plate and looked at Boase.

'Hungry, Archie?'

Bartlett stared at his wife.

'Princess, is that really a question you need to ask? I have never known this boy *not* to be hungry.'

'All right, sir.'

Boase fidgeted and Irene laughed again.

'Archie loves roast lamb, Mum – don't you, Archie?'

Bartlett snorted. 'Of course he does – it's food.'

Now everyone, including Boase, was laughing. Topper let out a sigh and rested his head on his paws, waiting for the first morsel to come his way.

Caroline Bartlett piled the first plate high with lamb, roast potatoes and vegetables.

'Well, I should thank you – I consider it an honour to see an empty plate. Here you are, Archie – tuck in. And Irene has made a lovely pudding, as usual.'

By two o'clock, the lunch was finished. Both men felt that they had eaten too much and Boase was in the scullery with Irene, washing up. Caroline sat down with some mending.

'Listen to those two, George. They seem so happy together. Do you think the wedding will be soon? Do you think it'll be next Easter – that seems to be what they'd like?'

'I have no idea, Princess. I hope they get their own place first – we don't really want them living here with us, do we?'

'I wouldn't mind, dear.'

'You forgotten what it was like living with your mother?'

'Well, no – I hadn't. I suppose it *was* rather trying.'

'And what if they want children? We couldn't cope with that at our age – anyway, there wouldn't be enough room...'

'George, I only asked about the wedding. Calm

161

down. Here, have another drop of beer and be quiet.'

Caroline topped up Bartlett's glass and carried on with her sewing.

'I saw that Mrs de Vere yesterday. She's a funny woman. I was behind her in the queue at the butcher's when I went in to pick up the lamb. She was complaining that her leg of lamb hadn't been such good quality as the one she had at Christmas and what were they going to do about it. Poor Joe Pentecost – he only started there last Saturday, straight from school too. She really gave him the run-around. Oh, but it was funny, George. She only came in to complain about the lamb. Joe went and fetched Mr Body because he didn't know how to deal with her. Mr Body refused to give her the money back, saying his lamb was the best in Cornwall and if she didn't want anything else he had a long queue of customers to serve. She was furious.'

'That's unusual for Ernest Body – he wouldn't say boo to a goose normally. It's about time someone stood up to that woman. She seems to think that just because she's got money she can do anything she likes.'

'Well, yes – but she usually can. Anyhow, when he told her to buy something or leave the shop she asked Joe Pentecost for two ounces of tongue.'

'Tongue? What was that for, the cat? I can't imagine Mrs de Vere eating tongue, can you, Princess?'

'Well, no, I can't. But she had to have the last word. Joe weighed the meat and wrapped it and as he handed it over the counter she flounced out and told Mr Body to have it sent round.'

'She's got a cheek.'

'Well, it then got worse because as she was flouncing, she didn't see Joe's bicycle leaning against the window as she left and tripped clean over it.'

'Did she hurt herself?'

'I'd say so – landed on her backside and they had to take her to the hospital.'

Bartlett laughed and couldn't stop laughing. As he continued, Boase and Irene came in from the scullery just in time to see Bartlett mopping his eyes with his handkerchief.

'George, dear – it's not that funny! Mr Body will never hear the last of this.'

Bartlett carried on laughing, then, when everyone thought he'd stopped, he laughed again. Caroline too began to giggle as she thought of Mrs de Vere lying on the pavement.

'What was everyone in the queue doing while all this was going on?'

'They were laughing, dear.'

Bartlett was now completely out of control and Topper sat up and put his paw on his master's knee.

'George, that's enough now – you're upsetting Topper.'

'I'm sorry, Topper, old man – I really needed that laugh. Come with me into the kitchen – let's see if we can find you a biscuit.'

The two left the room, Bartlett still chuckling to himself.

The Bank Holiday Monday passed uneventfully.

Bartlett spent the day in his garden and tried to relax. Boase took a walk over to Maenporth with his pocket sketchbook in search of some seabirds. He took a canvas bag which his landlady, Mrs Curgenven, had filled with a flask of tea, two ham sandwiches, a pork pie and some saffron cake.

Boase didn't eat much and he didn't paint much. He soon wandered over to the cave where Smith had held Irene. He thought over the case and couldn't understand why he felt bad about the whole thing. He was missing Irene – yes, he had only seen her yesterday but he wanted to see her *every* day. He wanted to wake up next to her, to bring her breakfast in bed, to sit with her at their own table and to fall asleep next to her. He skimmed some stones across the water and thought that he'd need a lot more money to provide a home for a wife. With no sketching done and almost as much food left as he had brought, Boase returned to Melvill Road and went to bed early.

'I didn't know Penhaligon had an interest in guns, Boase.'

'He did mention it to us before. You must have forgotten, sir. He was asking me before about what we used in the war – he's actually quite knowledgeable on the subject. Why?'

'Well, I just confiscated this.'

Bartlett slid a catalogue across the desk. Boase picked it up and flicked through it.

'Why did you take it off him?'

'Because he's supposed to be on duty – not reading unrelated material.'

Boase grinned, as there was a knock at the

door. Boase opened it to see Penhaligon with a tray of tea and some biscuits. Boase grinned all the more.

'Biscuits too? You must be after something, Penhaligon?'

'No, just thought you'd like some tea and a bit of something sweet, that's all.'

Boase held up the catalogue.

'Don't suppose you've come in for this?'

'Well, I would like it back.'

Bartlett looked up and over the top of his reading glasses.

'Don't let me catch you with that again, Penhaligon.'

'Yes, sir. Sorry, sir.'

Boase handed the offending article to Penhaligon.

'Just a minute, before you go, Penhaligon. Tell me what you know about weapons that might be used in a circus – say, for a lion tamer.'

'Well, what do you want to know?'

'What sort of gun would lion tamers have used, say before the war? Any idea?'

'They would have used any sort of pistol or revolver. Something small for ease of use, but something that could save their life with one shot if it had to.'

'Have you got any pictures in that catalogue of what they might have used before the war?'

'Yes, look, there's a whole history section they show every month at the back. Here you are, look at these pictures – there are lots here.'

Penhaligon flicked speedily through the catalogue.

'Wait – go back.'

Boase quickly leafed back through the pages. He snatched the catalogue from Penhaligon and looked hard at one picture in particular. The item that had caught his attention was a mahogany box. In a second picture the plush velvet interior was revealed showing two hand guns.

'I'm such an idiot.'

Bartlett looked up.

'What are you on about, Boase?'

'Me. I'm an idiot. Look at this – *a pair of guns!* Why didn't I think about that? Thanks for the tea, Penhaligon. Here's your catalogue.'

'Two guns – what of it?'

'Well, sir, what if Edward James' gun was one of an identical pair? I never even considered that.'

'Where would that leave us? I don't understand what you're getting at, Boase.'

'What I'm getting at is this. What if the gun that killed Clicker was one of an identical pair? Someone else could have had the other of the pair with the same bullets. Someone else could have killed the old man but laid the blame on James – or suspicion automatically fell on him.'

'I don't like this, Boase. I don't like what you're telling me. You're saying that this could be more proof that Edward James may not have killed the old man?'

'Well, you've doubted the verdict at turns, sir – you've been unsure in your mind that Greet did the right thing. In fact … you're absolutely positive that James was innocent.'

'Yes. Yes, I admit that. But this is a big thing you're saying, Boase. Anyway, how could you

166

prove it now?'

'There's only one way and that's to find the other gun.'

'How do you plan on doing that? Even if there was an identical one, even if you found it – none of that proves James' innocence. And what good would it do anyway?'

'It means that if we doubted it all before, yes, we can't bring Edward James back, but the killer is still at large ... which we've said to each other before. That's a big worry, sir.'

'Right – so who do you think this mystery person is then?'

'I don't know at the moment, obviously, sir.'

'You're going to rake up a lot of trouble with this.'

'If you don't want to be involved, I can do it on my own.'

'No. I can't give you the extra time to do that.'

'Oh.'

'And anyway, we're a team. So, where do we start?'

'Are you convinced then, sir?'

'I don't know what I am. But if we pursue this, we have to do it discreetly, and if we find nothing in fairly short order then we abandon the whole thing. Not a word to Greet about this either. Understood?'

'Understood, sir. Thank you, sir.'

'Don't thank me. I must be mad. If your theory is proved to be right, I don't know what we'll do about it.'

'Cross that bridge when we come to it?'

'Deal.'

Archie Boase walked along Hunter's Path. The moon was full and lit his way. He hadn't been able to sleep and, as he often did when this happened, had got out of bed, dressed, raided the pantry for some 'eatables' as he called his snack foods and walked towards the sea front. He had already walked in the shadow of Pendennis Castle and passed the spot where Clicker had been found dead. For some reason, he now retraced his steps and visited that place again. Maybe there would be something else to see, something else to discover. He thought how stupid this was, here in the dark with only momentary and sporadic beams from the moon and with the death of Clicker weeks away and probably any evidence that might have been, gone with the time and the elements. In any case, they had searched and searched this site and found nothing of any use.

As Boase stooped low and examined the ground with the aid of his torch, he heard something move quite close to him. He stood still and listened. There it was again. He turned quickly and shone the torch into the hedge just in time to see a feral cat staring at him, its eyes sparkling like jewels in the narrow beam of light. Boase smiled to himself and pulled a pork pie from his pocket. As he began to eat, looking up at the moon, he was aware that he was still being watched. He regarded the cat. It stared back. Boase pulled a piece of meat from the pie and threw it in the cat's direction. The cat pushed it head through the brambles and gratefully took the morsel. It looked at Boase again, expectantly and Boase crumbled the last of the pie and lay it on the ground near to where the cat waited. He pushed the empty bag back into his pocket and walked away, looking back to see the cat taking the pie. He smiled and thought how he loved animals and nature and, well, this beautiful planet in general. Then he thought about the people that marred it with their nastiness and greed and cruelty. As he mused over this he reached the Falmouth Hotel and, slipping down a side road next to the imposing building, made his way back home.

'I've just heard the circus is leaving tonight, Boase. If you've got anything you want to say to any of them you'd better do it today.'

'Yes I have, sir. I've just got a couple of things to do and then I thought I'd go up there. Coming?'

'I think I will – they've almost become a part of the furniture, they've been here so long. There are a couple of people I want to say goodbye to – particularly the Warner girls.'

'I've got a feeling they won't want to say goodbye to us though, sir.'

'You may be right – but I'll try. Anyway, look, Greet wants to see me – he's getting right on my nerves, he is, straight. I won't be long.'

True to his word, Bartlett wasn't very long. He came back into the office ten minutes later and sat behind his desk.

'You all right, sir – what did he want?'

'To tell me about Molly James. She's been hanged. This morning.'

Bartlett lit his pipe and looked out of the

window onto the street below.

'Well, we knew they'd do it, sir. There was no doubt about her at least, was there?'

'No. No, there was no doubt. But even so, whether there is doubt or not, well...'

'Say it, sir. Say what's on your mind.'

'Well, it's not exactly civilised, is it? An eye for an eye. And then we're taught two wrongs don't make a right. I don't know, Boase – I'm getting too old for this caper. When I was young, I thought the death penalty was a good thing, they got what they deserved.'

'And now?'

'Now, I wonder how civilised we actually are. To murder someone legally – that's what Irene calls it, "legalised murder".'

'Do you think they'll ever stop doing it, sir?'

'I don't know the answer to that, my boy. Not in my lifetime, I'm sure. Maybe one day they'll see sense and find a better way. Anyway, I can't sit here all day gossiping. What's done is done. Now, about this gun business – let's talk more about that, have a cup of tea and get up to see off the circus.'

Chapter Thirteen

At half past four, Bartlett and Boase arrived at the recreation ground. The caravans had been made ready and most were lined up in preparation to leave. Arthur Wayland was soothing his

170

lions, who were pacing back and forth anxiously. Bartlett walked over to him.

'Good evening, Arthur. All ready?'

'Hello, Mr Bartlett, sir. Yes, yes, I think we're all ready to move off soon. The cats don't like travelling so much – I've just given them a little something to calm them down a bit.'

'Where's your first stop?'

'I'm not sure, Plymouth maybe.'

'Well, I wish you a safe trip.'

'Thanks, Mr Bartlett. This has all left a nasty taste in my mouth.'

'And in mine, Arthur. Tell me – what's happening to Clicker's caravan?'

'Well, I think it's been cleared out and we're just taking it along with us. Mr Martin will probably allocate it to someone else. It didn't belong to Clicker – it's circus property.'

'I see. Do you know where the Warner girls are at the moment?'

'I think they're still in their caravan packing.'

'Thanks – I just want to nip over and see them, to say goodbye.'

'Righto, Mr Bartlett, sir. Thanks for everything.'

'All the best, Arthur.'

Bartlett and Boase walked across to the Warner caravan and Boase knocked at the door. Betty Warner opened it and stared hard at Boase.

'Oh, it's you. What do you want?'

'Well, Miss Warner, we came to say goodbye and to offer our very sincere condolences.'

Boase turned his hat over in his hands, expecting a stream of abuse to come hurtling his way, but it didn't. Betty sighed.

171

'Do you want to come in for a moment?'

'Yes, thank you.'

Boase followed by Bartlett walked up the small steps and entered the caravan. Joan Warner was packing a small bag on the kitchen table. She smiled at the two men. Betty indicated a bench seat under the window and Bartlett and Boase sat down.

'I'm afraid I can't offer you any tea – the kettle has been packed.'

Bartlett loosened his collar.

'That's quite all right – we can't stay. We just wanted to come and say sorry for all your trouble.'

'That's kind of you – thank you. We miss Anne so terribly. Life just won't be the same again, Inspector Bartlett.'

Betty's voice cracked as she spoke.

'Well, I'm very sorry we weren't able to prevent what happened to her.'

'And we're sorry we blamed you. It wasn't your fault.'

'I hope you can find some peace in your lives, both of you.'

'Thanks. We're going to carry on here for the next few weeks then we may return home – maybe try to find a normal job. Anne hated doing this – if we had tried to get out before then she might still be here.'

'Well, you can't really think like that – although I understand completely.'

Bartlett stood up.

'We should be going. We just wanted to see you before you left.'

Betty offered her hand to Bartlett and then to

Boase. Both shook it warmly. Joan smiled and carried on packing. Boase looked out of the small window.

'Oh, looks like the first caravans are moving.'

Betty looked outside.

'Yes, ours will be going soon. Thank you both for coming. It was really very kind of you.'

Bartlett and Boase stepped outside. Bartlett paused to light his pipe and Boase wandered over to watch the first few caravans being taken out to the road. He recognised Clicker's and watched the empty caravan being pushed along by two young men in order to hitch it to a trailer. As the caravan was pulled further across the grass, Boase stared hard. Something didn't look right. He stooped to the ground and stared again at the caravan from this angle. Suddenly he shouted out.

'Hey, you! Stop – wait.'

Boase ran across to the two men with Clicker's caravan. Bartlett, astonished, followed him across the grass. He caught up with Boase at the caravan and watched as he crawled underneath. Pointing his pipe in Boase's direction, he addressed the two young men.

'You be sure and hold that steady – I don't want that dropped on him, mind.'

The two men and Bartlett watched as Boase crawled back out from under the caravan clutching a wooden box. He stood up.

'What's that, Boase?'

Boase looked at the two men who were staring at him and, grabbing Bartlett's sleeve, drew the older man away.

173

'Well?'

'I haven't opened it but ... this looks remarkably like a gun box to me.'

'*What?*'

Boase had taken his penknife from his pocket and was already prising open the box. He lifted the lid and showed the inside to Bartlett.

'It's empty, sir.'

'Well – what does that mean, Boase? Why was it under the caravan?'

'I'm guessing it was hidden there or put there for safekeeping. Look inside, there should be two guns, look at the apertures – I'd say the gun we took from Edward James would fit nicely into here...'

'And the other?'

'Who knows? But, Penhaligon was right – these things often came in pairs and it looks like Clicker had something to do with them.'

'Do you think he knew this was under his caravan?'

'Well, that's the next thing – I don't know the answer to that.'

'So, let me see if I'm getting this right, Boase. Edward James had a gun which incriminated him for the murder of Clicker...'

'Well, amongst other evidence, yes.'

'Right. Now you're telling me that there were two guns, both of them were originally in this case, and Edward James had one of them?'

'Exactly so – that's my opinion, sir.'

'So, who had the other one?'

'Don't know.'

'But whoever it was could have killed Clicker

and incriminated James?'

'That's possible – isn't it?'

'I had a bad feeling about this, Boase. A bad feeling.'

'But don't forget there was other evidence against James too, sir.'

'Yes, but that wasn't exactly watertight, was it? I mean, a fake witness statement from a man who had an axe to grind and freely admitted he'd stop at nothing to get back at Edward James. That, along with some other bits of information which I now distrust highly doesn't make for a solid case. Greet! I despair of that man, Boase, he's been at the root of this all along. I said he was being too hasty but would he have it? No. He would not. Oh, dear me. What a terrible mess. Well, he's going to have to be told about this.'

'You're not going to tell him really, are you, sir?'

'I'll have to. Not only may he have had an innocent man put to death but it means someone else could be running around like a lunatic with this other gun.'

'I suppose so, sir.'

Bartlett, with Boase still carrying the wooden box made their way back to the station to tell Greet what they had found.

Bartlett sat in his chair tapping his fingers on the desk. He was angry.

'What did he say, sir?'

Bartlett looked up.

'He said it's all *my* fault and I'm to sort it out.'

'Crikey – no wonder you're angry, sir. Anything I can do?'

'I don't even know what *I* can do – Greet's caused all this mess and now I'm supposed to put it right. What does he expect me to do – bring a man back from the dead?'

'I'm sorry, sir. What exactly did he say?'

'Well, he had plenty to say, believe me, but mainly that we had to find out where the other gun was and investigate its current owner.'

'Well, that's easier said than done.'

'You're damned right. What a business. What a terrible mess – and he's left it all to me.'

'No, sir – he's left it all to *us*. I'm partly to blame for raking all this over about the guns.'

'No, no you're not – it was the right thing to do. The wrong thing to do was to let him take over the case – it's all about speed and statistics with him, all the time. What happened to good, old-fashioned policing, eh?'

'Don't worry, sir. We'll put it right – we have to now, because we can't leave someone at large with that other gun.'

'No, quite, but where do we start? Just look how much trouble that man's caused, Boase. He's got the cheek to go on and on at me that it's about time I thought about hanging up my boots – well, he should bury his ... preferably while he's still wearing them.'

'Sir!' Boase was startled by this unusual outburst by Bartlett.

'Well, you must feel the same, Boase. What started off as a clown being subjected to extortion could have been nipped in the bud in all probability – now look, it's literally turned into a circus and not in a good way.'

176

'Well, you know what they say, sir.'

'What?'

'A fool and his money...'

'Go and fetch some tea, Boase, before I clobber you.'

Bartlett was grinning, glad of some light relief, but inside he was in turmoil. How would he solve this problem?

'Have you got anything for the church fête, Mum?'

Irene Bartlett was preparing a basket of food to take to the church. Topper had been eagerly following her in and out of the garden as she brought in vegetables.

'Topper – as far as I know, you don't eat raw vegetables. OK – try a bit of carrot.'

Irene handed the dog a piece of the vegetable and he took it gently from her. Giving her a puzzled look, he dropped it instantly onto the floor.

'See ... I knew you wouldn't like it. Wait a minute and I'll go and get you a biscuit. Would you like that?'

Caroline was in the kitchen and took down a large tin from a shelf. Topper wagged his tail – this was *his* very own tin.

'Here you are, boy. She's horrible, isn't she, to give you raw carrot?'

Topper took the biscuit and ran out into the garden.

'Here you are, Irene – here's a nice turnip, too. That should be enough to take. Will you be able to carry this? It's rather heavy now.'

'I'll be fine, Mum.'

'Is Archie coming again soon, dear? I'm sure you two don't spend nearly enough time together?'

'Well, Archie's busy, Mum. You know Dad's having trouble with all this circus business.'

'Yes, dear. All the same, I know you love being together – maybe you should try to find the time.'

'Maybe, Mum. I've got to go past the station – shall I look in and invite him for tea tomorrow?'

'Why not, dear? That would be nice.'

'Right. I'm going to be late, Mum. See you later.'

'Be careful, Irene dear.'

Irene slipped her coat around her shoulders, kissed her mother and left for the church. Having dropped off the basket, she carried on to the police station and went inside. Ernest Penhaligon was at the desk.

'Good morning, Miss Bartlett. Would you like to see your father?'

'Well, just quickly, Ernie. Is Archie with him?'

'Yes, I think so.'

Constable Penhaligon led Irene to Bartlett's office and knocked on the door. Boase opened it.

'Irene! How nice to see you – what brings you here?'

'Hello, Archie, hello, Dad.'

Bartlett stood up as his daughter entered the room.

'Hello, Irene – is your mother all right?'

'She's fine, Dad. I just came to ask Archie if he'd like to come for tea tomorrow. Archie?'

'That'd be lovely, Irene. Thank you.'

178

'Right, must dash. 'Bye, Archie. 'Bye, Dad.'

'That girl wears me out sometimes, Boase – hope you're going to be able to keep up with her, my boy.'

'I'm sure I'll manage, sir.'

Boase grinned widely as he thought how he couldn't wait to have Irene completely to himself – yes, he thought the world of her parents but this was one person he didn't feel like sharing.

'Boase, call Penhaligon in here, will you?'

Boase went and fetched the constable and the three men sat in the office.

Bartlett drew out the empty gun box from his desk drawer. From another locked drawer he pulled the gun that had been used as evidence in the case against Edward James.

Boase was astonished to see the gun again.

'Where did you get that from, sir?'

'I took the precaution of requesting it from the property store in Bodmin to see if it fits in this box. If it doesn't, it isn't a twin.'

He laid the open box on the top of his desk and slowly tried to fit the gun inside. Boase and Penhaligon watched. The weapon dropped firmly into the padded aperture. Penhaligon jumped up.

'Where did you find that, sir? I haven't seen one of these since I was a boy.'

'We, or rather, Boase, found it under Clicker's caravan when the circus was leaving. I didn't want to say anything until I confirmed that this weapon came from this box. You were just telling us about these pairs of guns and, would you believe, this has turned up?'

179

Penhaligon picked up the box and ran his fingers over the gun.

'So, do we know where the other one is, sir?'

'No, Penhaligon, unfortunately we don't – could be anywhere but I'm more than a little worried what it might be used for next.'

Boase looked at Bartlett.

'But … isn't this all over now, sir?'

'You carry on, Penhaligon – thanks.'

Penhaligon left and Bartlett closed the gun box, leaving the gun inside.

'It's all over if the real killer has been brought to justice. But … well, if Greet has been too hasty, which isn't beyond the realms of possibility, then, well, I really don't know what to say or do.'

'But it all fits though, sir – doesn't it?'

'Greet thinks so.'

'Well, maybe we just have to take it on the chin then.'

Bartlett sighed heavily and looked out of the window.

'I've had enough of this place for today, Boase. I'm all in – think I'll cut along and take Topper out to Swanpool. Fancy coming along?'

'No thanks, sir – I've still got quite a lot to get through here. The amount of paperwork is ridiculous. While I think of it – when are we getting our police uniforms back? We *are* police, after all.'

'Well, Greet wants us to stay in plain clothes when we're on a big case – insists the uniform scares people off. As you say – we *are* police but ours is not to reason why. Goodnight, Boase. Don't work on too long.'

'Goodnight, sir. See you in the morning.'

Bartlett felt relieved to be out of the station, more relieved to be away from Greet. The days seemed to be getting longer for him. Maybe Greet was right. Maybe he *was* getting too old. Well, things would all look a lot better when he saw his beloved Caroline – and Topper, of course. As Bartlett approached his house in Penmere Hill he could distinctly hear a dog barking frantically. As he walked on he realised it was Topper. He walked quicker, then ran through the gate and up the path. He fumbled for his keys as he could see Topper through the frosted glass, jumping up and down, still barking.

'I'm coming, Topper. It's OK, boy. It's me.'

The dog went quiet. As Bartlett turned the key he realised he couldn't push the door. He looked down and could see Caroline's foot against the skirting board.

'Oh no! It's all right, Topper. Wait there.'

Bartlett ran down the lane at the end of the terrace and around to the back gate, running across the garden. He tried the scullery door. It was bolted. He pulled off his coat and wrapped it around his arm. Shielding his face, he broke the glass in the door and drew back the bolt. He ran through the house and to the front door where Caroline was slumped on the floor. He picked her up and listened for her breath. It was there but shallow.

'Oh, Princess, oh no! What's happened? Please wake up.'

Caroline opened her eyes.

'George. Is that you?'

181

'Of course it's me, my beautiful Princess. Oh, you gave me the fright of my life. What happened? Where's Irene?'

'I think I just fainted, George. Irene's gone to buy some meat for Topper – she should be back soon.'

'Caroline, I can't keep leaving you alone like this.'

'I'm not usually alone, George, dear. I've got Irene most of the time.'

'Yes, but Irene will be married soon and it's unlikely that she'll still be living here then – then I won't be able to go to work and leave you. Do you feel able to get up now? I'll make you some tea.'

Caroline took Bartlett's hand and tried to stand up. Immediately she fell back down.

'Princess – let me help you. Come on now.'

Bartlett bent down and gently lifted his wife up. He couldn't help noticing how small she felt in his arms. Slowly, and followed by Topper, he took her into the parlour and laid her carefully onto the couch.

'Now, don't you go anywhere, I'll make us both a cuppa.'

'I'm not going anywhere, George.'

Topper lay on the floor next to the couch. He stood up when Bartlett returned with a tray of tea and some biscuits.

'Now, here's some tea and something sweet – I bet you've had nothing to eat today. Here's one for you, Topper, old man. Here you are now – that's for doing such good work and looking after your mother. So, Princess. Have you eaten today?'

'I had some toast this morning.'

'But that was hours and hours ago. Why didn't Irene make you some lunch?'

'I wasn't really hungry, dear. I'm fine now, thank you. Thank you for looking after me.'

Caroline patted her husband's hand and he leaned forward and kissed her cheek.

'Well, this isn't the first time you've been taken ill like this. I want you to see the doctor again.'

'George, I only fainted.'

'Well, that's as maybe, but what if you had banged your head when you fell? I dread to think what might have happened. I want you to see the doctor – and I won't take no for an answer.'

Chapter Fourteen

Dr Clemo sat behind the desk in his surgery. He looked at George and Caroline Bartlett.

'Mrs Bartlett, as you are aware, I have just taken over the running of this surgery. I have looked at your medical notes and your history and, having examined you, I feel that the best thing that you could do for your health is to rest. Completely.'

'But I *do* rest, Doctor. I have a nap every afternoon and my daughter does most things around the house.'

'But it's not enough, Mrs Bartlett. In your frail condition I am going to recommend that you take at least two weeks off and away from the family home. It is entirely up to you of course whether you choose to take that advice. Mr Bartlett, it would be highly recommended that you went with your wife. I would prefer that she had someone to take care of her at all times.'

'But, Doctor, my husband is a working man. He can't just take time off from that, he's very busy.'

'As I said, Mrs Bartlett, that's your choice, but I am your doctor now and that is my professional opinion. Mr Bartlett, you would be wise to take my advice if you want your wife to enjoy good health. "Nervous exhaustion" is what we call it and, without rest and recuperation, things generally tend to become worse.'

Bartlett was listening intently. 'I understand perfectly, Doctor. Thank you. I will see to it that my wife gets exactly everything she needs.'

Bartlett helped Caroline with her coat and, thanking Dr Clemo, the couple left the surgery.

'George, dear. This really isn't necessary. We can't just go away. I'm perfectly all right at home.'

'This is not your decision this time, Princess. If the doctor says you need rest away from here then that's what you shall have. I'll tell Greet that I need compassionate leave. He can go to the devil.'

'George!'

'I'm sorry, Princess ... right, I want you to decide where you would like to go. You don't need to worry about work. I'll take you somewhere quiet and you can relax.'

'But, George, what about Irene? We can't leave her.'

'Oh yes we can. Irene is an independent young woman, soon to be married. She'll insist when she knows it's for the good of your health. And anyway, I'll get Boase to keep an eye on her. You don't need to worry about them.'

'Well, if you're sure. I don't want to be a burden.'

'And I don't want to see you making yourself ill. You gave me such a fright yesterday. Now, behave and do as you're told.'

Bartlett had little trouble in convincing Greet that he needed to be away, and no trouble at all having the same conversation with Boase.

'Of course you must go, if that's what the doctor has recommended, sir. You don't need to worry about Irene – I can look in every evening, make sure she's safe and that the house is secure. Irene is the least of your worries, I promise.'

'That's good to know, Boase – Caroline has been fretting so much about her. I've managed to find us a little cottage at Perranporth. Just for one week – she wouldn't stay any longer, but that's better than nothing.'

'Might do you both good, sir.'

'Yes, well ... Greet is up to something. Jumped at the chance to be rid of me. Keep an eye on him, Boase. He's shifty.'

Boase grinned. 'Will do, sir.'

True to his word, on the first evening, Boase called in at the Bartlett house. Irene was having some supper.

'Come in, Archie. You really don't need to look

after me. I'm fine, really I am.'

'Irene, I promised your parents. Now, is that enough for you to eat? It doesn't look very much to me.'

'Well, it *wouldn't* look much to you, would it? You're *always* eating.'

Boase laughed and drew Irene nearer to him to kiss her.

'I can't wait until we're on our own, in our own house, Irene. I just can't wait.'

'I know. Me neither. Now look, Archie Boase, you don't need to hang around – I'm perfectly fine. Go on now, I'm sure you've got an early start tomorrow – and you need to cover for Dad too, so you'll be busy.'

'Well, if you're sure.'

'I'm sure.'

'Well, let me hear you bolt the door when I leave – and take Topper upstairs with you.'

Boase pulled Irene to him and kissed her again.

'I don't want to leave you on your own.'

'Just go, Archie. I've got Topper – he'll look after me.'

'Goodnight, Irene.'

'Goodnight, Archie.'

Irene closed the door and giggled as Boase opened the letterbox and called through it.

'Don't forget the bolt – I'm waiting.'

She secured the door and went to bed.

Irene didn't know what had woken her up. The moon shone a beam of light through a gap in the curtains and, using that, she looked at the little clock beside the bed. It was ten past two. She looked down beside the bed. Topper was sitting up and looking at the door. Irene whispered to him.

'What is it, Topper? Did you hear something, boy?'

She put her hand on Topper's collar and felt the hairs stiffening on his neck. He let out a low growl. Irene walked slowly to the door. She peered out onto the landing and went downstairs, Topper closely at her heels. Her heart was racing. She heard a loud crash in the back garden and Topper, hearing it too, ran to the kitchen, barking loudly. Irene followed and tried to look through the window. The moon had disappeared and Irene could see nothing. She was shaking now. She sat on the kitchen floor with her arms around Topper and sobbed.

'Topper, I think we should go and get Archie. Come on, boy.'

She pulled on her coat over her pyjamas and a pair of gumboots which were in the hall. She clipped Topper's lead onto his collar and slowly drew back the bolt. Cautiously she looked about her and went out into the front garden. Closing the door behind her, she and Topper made their way up Penmere Hill and on towards Melvill Road. Reaching Boase's lodgings, in a moment of calm, she thought to herself how stupid she must look, although she had seen no one on her way here. More importantly, how was she going to let Archie know that she was here? She couldn't just knock at the door and risk waking Mrs Curgenven. As she paused by the gate, Topper began to wag his tail and let out a joyful whine, followed by a little bark. He wagged his tail faster as the object of his affection came into view across the lawn.

'Irene? Is that you? What on earth...?'

Irene spun round to see Boase jump across the front garden wall and onto the pavement.

'Archie! You almost frightened the life out of me. What are you doing here at this time of night?'

'It is I who should be surprised to see you – and in your nightclothes too. What on earth has happened, Irene?'

Boase put his arm around his girl and held her close. Suddenly feeling secure, Irene now felt not a little embarrassed.

'Promise you won't laugh?'

'Tell me.'

'I woke up – and Topper woke up too. We both heard a noise in the garden and we went down to see what it was. Well, then, I got a bit scared and decided to come and find you. I thought I'd be OK on my own ... and I was until I heard that.'

Boase hugged her tighter.

'Well, you might have put some day clothes on first. Come on, I'll take you back.'

'Archie?'

'Yes, my love?'

'You haven't explained why you're out here.'

'Well, believe it or not, I couldn't sleep and I got worried about you. So I was about to come over to see if you were all right, make sure the house was secure.'

'It is. You saw for yourself. But thank you. I'm so glad you thought about me.'

'I'm always thinking about you, Irene.'

They made their way back to Penmere. Boase went inside with Irene.

'Go on. You go up to bed – I'm not leaving you alone tonight. I'll sleep down here on the couch.'

'I can't let you do that, Archie. I'll be fine now.'

'Don't you want me here?'

'Of course I do. I love having you near me – you make me feel safe.'

'Then go on – off to bed. You've still got time to get some sleep.'

Boase kissed Irene and settled down on the couch.

'Shall I get you a blanket, Archie?'

'No. It's not cold. Goodnight, Irene.'

'Goodnight, Archie – and thank you.'

Boase, feeling extremely weary, left the Bartlett house and went home to change into his work clothes. He grabbed a few things from the pantry and shoved them into his pocket for later. By nine o'clock he was sitting at his desk. He yawned and delved into his pocket. He drew out two paper bags; one contained a slice of veal and ham pie, the other, a large piece of cheese. Deciding that this fare would be far too dry, he went in search of tea.

As he reached the lobby he bumped into Penhaligon.

'Good morning, Penhaligon – I was looking for tea?'

'Well, as luck would have it, I've just made some. Shall I bring it in?'

'No, I'll come and get it. Boase followed Penhaligon to a small kitchen area and poured himself a cup of tea.

'Oh. A letter arrived for you this morning, Archie. I'll fetch it for you.'

Seconds later, Boase was tearing open the envelope. He carefully read the contents.

Dear Boase,
Please let Irene know that we've arrived here safely and that we are both well.

Boase, I've been thinking – about our case. I can't let this rest. I want you to do something for me. I'm already bored out of my mind here and it's only day one but you realise I have to do this for Caroline – otherwise I would come with you.

I want you to go back to Hunter's Path – where Clicker was found. Don't tell anyone where you are going and be sure to go alone. Go during daylight hours. There is something. I don't know what it is, but there is something. Maybe a small clue we overlooked: Greet isn't the world's best sleuth, but you, Boase – well, you've got a good brain. Search until you find something. I know you're busy but there's a definite whiff of haddock in the air and I mean to get to the bottom of this.

Be sure Greet doesn't discover what you're doing. If you find anything, please God you do, then let me know when I return. I'll be back on the 25th.

Take care of Irene.
All the best
George Bartlett

Boase took his tea back to his office and re-read Bartlett's letter. What was the old man up to? He must have posted this yesterday as soon as he had arrived at Perranporth. Boase couldn't help

190

thinking that this was turning into a vendetta against Greet. There had been two murders and, as far as most people could see, two people were fairly tried and paid the penalty for the crimes. Boase didn't really understand what Bartlett was asking him to do. He respected his superior but couldn't see why he was dragging this whole affair out. He finished the tea and took a bite out of the pie. He stuck his head around the door and called Penhaligon into his office.

'Penhaligon, come in a moment. Is Greet in today?'

'Not until two o'clock, I think. Let me just check to be sure.'

Penhaligon disappeared and returned with the station diary.

'No, my mistake. Three o'clock – look, here.'

'Even better.'

'Pardon?'

'Nothing, Penhaligon. Look, I've got to go out on an errand for Inspector Bartlett but I don't want anyone to know I'm doing it.'

'Bit secretive is it?'

Penhaligon was grinning.

'Seriously, Penhaligon. No one has seen me yet except you. Keep it that way. I'm going out now and I'll be back as soon as I can. You haven't seen me – right?'

'Right. No problem. See you later.'

Boase took his coat and left the station to investigate Hunter's Path in accordance with Bartlett's wishes.

Boase decided to take full advantage of Greet's

absence and took a walk across the seafront. He paused a couple of times to observe a few boats on the water then went up to Pendennis Castle and headed for the moat. Once there he walked part way around the moat wondering what he was looking for, when he eventually came nearer to the murder site. He wanted to be clear in his mind before he looked again. What was Bartlett thinking? What had they missed? Boase couldn't get anything straight in his head and so carried on walking until he reached the place of the clown's murder.

Boase spent an hour here. He felt as though he had turned over every blade of grass, every leaf, every stone. He wiped his forehead and pushed back his hair. There was nothing. He sat down and reached for the piece of cheese in his pocket. He felt so tired. Now he was letting Bartlett down – or was he? There never was going to be anything. They'd been thorough. Greet said he'd been over the ground again afterwards. Bartlett would just have to accept that it was over.

Boase ate his cheese and lay back against the grassy bank under a tree. The weak autumn sun felt relaxing on his face. He closed his eyes and listened to the seagulls chattering as they soared above him, listened to the wind rustling the last of the leaves in the trees and decided that going over old ground was fruitless. He fell asleep.

A while later he stirred, still half asleep. Yet awake enough to be churning events over in his mind. No point going over old ground ... old ground. He opened his eyes. The sun had disappeared and now the wind was whipping across his face. He lay there for a moment or two. As he watched the autumn leaves tumbling from the trees he was reminded he was laying in the exact spot where Clicker had been found. He couldn't waste any more time on this, he'd have to go back to the station. Bartlett would be disappointed. At that moment Boase heard two seagulls fighting above his head. As he watched them his eyes were drawn closer to the tree. He was staring now. What was that in the branches? Something was swaying to and fro above him. He looked harder. No! It couldn't be – how on earth...?

Chapter Fifteen

Boase stood at the foot of the tree, looking up. He needed to climb the precarious branches to retrieve what he had just seen – what had just become visible amongst the few remaining leaves which had been clinging on to life since the summer months had come to an end and autumn had arrived. He *had* to get up there. This could be what Bartlett had asked him for. But, even George Bartlett could never have expected this. *Never*. If Boase's eyes weren't deceiving him from his position on the ground under that sparse tree, well, this could change everything and cause untold trouble.

Boase began to climb. As he reached the object of his interest, he lunged forward and attempted to grab it from the branch. Suddenly, with the shift in his weight, the branch he had been standing on snapped and Boase tumbled to the ground. The pain seared through his right ankle and lower leg. He lay on the grass, unable to move. He looked up again – he had been so close. *Now what?* As he lay there thinking how he could get back up – and he had to get back up there for Bartlett, he heard voices. He tried to sit up as a young girl came into view. She was running in Boase's direction, laughing. Soon, a young man came running up. He grabbed the girl and kissed her. Neither of them had seen Boase. The girl was giggling and the man kissed her again and, laying his coat at his feet, pulled her down onto the bank.

'Oh, no.'

Boase was muttering under his breath. He didn't want to see any more. He really didn't. He coughed. He coughed again. The girl looked across and let out a small squeal.

'Teddy – look. There's a man over there.'

Teddy, irritated at the intrusion, looked at Boase. He got up immediately and ran across the grass. He looked at Boase.

'I say! Are you all right, old man? What happened to you?'

This was the last thing Boase wanted. How to explain this now?

'I'm not really sure – I think I must have tripped over something and I fell.'

The man looked about him.

'Well, I don't see anything here, old sport. What say I help you up?'

'No – really, thanks but I'm fine. I can manage.'

Too late. The man was already pulling Boase to

his feet – with some difficulty, Boase being at least six inches taller and of a bigger build than his rescuer. Boase tried to stand, all the while hoping that the man wouldn't look up into the tree; that he could never explain. Boase straightened himself and brushed off his coat.

'That's very kind of you – I can manage now. Thank you.'

The man remained. Boase coughed.

'Really, you don't need to worry.'

'Can I give you a lift – back into the town maybe? That ankle is beginning to swell up, you'll have trouble walking on it. I'm a doctor by the way –Teddy Bennett.'

Bennett held out his hand and Boase shook it.

'Archie Boase. Really, Dr Bennett, I can manage.'

A gust of wind blew still more leaves down from the tree and Boase twitched visibly at the thought of his find being discovered by anyone but him – he could never explain that. Luckily, Teddy's girl was impatient.

'Teddy, come on, darling. The gentleman has told you he doesn't need help. Let's go.'

'All right, Felicity, I'm coming.'

The doctor patted Boase on the back and walked off towards Felicity. He turned and waved and Boase waved back, relieved that the pair had gone. That could have been disastrous, he thought.

Boase looked up again. How could he get back into the tree? He could barely walk, so bad was the pain. He took a few paces towards the trunk and, scrabbling to get a hold with his fingers, put his left foot up, the bark crumbling beneath his shoe, then the right one. The pain cut him like a knife. He couldn't stop now. Not now he'd seen this – Bartlett was right and this had to be sorted out. He climbed a little higher, beads of sweat forming on his brow. He stopped to rest, hardly believing what had just happened – he hadn't fallen out of a tree since he was six. His breath returned, he climbed again and reached almost the same spot as before. The original branch lying on the ground beneath him, he reached for another. Now he could reach ... he had to reach. He extended his arm. Another branch cracked. He stretched again and dragged the object towards himself. He heaved a sigh of relief. Slowly now he began the descent. As he reached the ground, he stumbled and fell down. He looked at his ankle. Yes, it was swollen – and very painful. Boase didn't know how he would make the walk back but, for now, he had to examine what he had just discovered.

Boase sat for ten minutes with the gun in his lap. It was attached to a sort of rubberised, stretchy band. Boase pulled the band. It was able to be extended a good few feet, he thought. He examined the gun. One bullet was missing. Boase now had an idea about this but didn't want to believe what he was thinking. He didn't want to imagine telling Bartlett what he thought. He didn't want to imagine Bartlett telling Greet what he thought.

He spent over an hour walking back to Melvill Road. He went inside and slowly climbed the stairs to his room. He took off his shoe and, rolling up his trouser leg, looked at his ankle. The swelling was really bad now – but hopefully just a sprain. As he sat wondering how to deal with this problem he heard a noise against the window, a volley of pebbles. He went over and looked down into the garden. It was Irene. He pulled up the window and leaned out.

'Irene – what's up. Are you OK?'

'I'm fine, Archie – I didn't know if you'd be in. I forgot that Dad left an address for you. He said you might need it if you wanted to contact him while he's away.'

'I do need to contact him actually, Irene. I'll come down – I might be a while.'

Boase carefully negotiated the stairs and opened the front door. As he walked out into the garden, Irene ran to him.

'Archie – what on earth has happened to you? Oh, you poor dear.'

'Would you believe I fell out of a tree?'

'Aren't you a bit old for climbing trees?'

'Well, yes, but don't ask questions now, please, Irene. I need to get a message to your father. I need to write him a letter – will he get it tomorrow?'

'Archie – if it's urgent, send him a telegram!'

'Oh, yes, I hadn't thought of that.'

Irene smiled.

'Shall I do it for you – you can't walk with your ankle so bad?'

'If you like – but I have to be at work tomorrow. I'll just try and rest it; it's probably only a sprain. Look, all you need to do is send this message – that is, if you wouldn't mind.'

'I offered, didn't I?'

Boase drew a piece of paper and a pencil from his pocket and wrote a short message on it. He gave it to Irene and she looked at it.

'What's wrong, Archie? This says you've found something that Dad needs to know about. Is everything all right?'

'Yes, don't worry, but I'll be very glad when your father returns home.'

'Well, if I go now, I should just be in time to send this. Why don't you come over later and I'll make you some food? If you can walk, that is?'

'Well, yes, that would be lovely. Thanks.'

'Come at about seven then?'

'Will do. Thanks, Irene. See you later.'

Irene left Boase and went to send the telegram.

Boase took remedial action with his injury and walked slowly to the Bartlett house; it felt painful as he walked and he began to limp more but nothing would keep him from his girl. Irene was waiting at the gate and she ran up the road to meet him. She slipped her arm through his.

'Archie, that looks very bad. You should get someone at the hospital to look at it.'

'Irene, please stop fussing.'

Irene looked up at him and he kissed her forehead. She squeezed his arm.

'Promise me that if it gets any worse, you'll get someone to deal with it? You can't go to work like this, you can barely walk.'

'Irene, please. I promise – and yes, I can. I'm sure it'll be better by then.'

The pair made their way up the path to the

front door. Topper was waiting on the other side and barked excitedly as the pair entered the hall.

'Topper, stop that. Archie has hurt himself and he doesn't want you making a racket. Go on. Go and lie in your bed.'

Irene put some cushions on a sofa in the parlour.

'Sit down, Archie – here, let me help you.'

'Irene, please, I'm not an invalid. I don't need to sit down – or cushions. I need this.'

Boase put his arms around Irene's waist and drew her to him. He kissed her on the cheek and rubbed the side of his face against her hair. He could smell lilacs.

'Do you love me, Irene?'

'Archie ... of course I do. You know that.'

'Then ditto.' He kissed her again.

The two of them sat in the parlour and ate some cold food. When they had eaten Boase put his arm around her.

'We should think about where we're going to live when we're married. Got any thoughts?'

'Well, I've thought about it quite a lot actually. I'm not sure we can afford our own place straight away. Mum and Dad...'

'No, Irene. I think the world of your parents but I'm not living here with them. I want you all to myself.'

'But it *would* be practical ... maybe just for six months.'

'No, Irene, and that's that. Anything else is up to you but I can't agree with that. We can afford somewhere small. Why don't you have a proper look over the next couple of weeks and then, nearer the time of the wedding, we'll know how much these things cost. And, about the wedding – we really should decide on a date.'

'Archie – you're so bossy, you make me laugh. We haven't really had time to discuss it, you're always working and busy.'

'Well, let's make time. You can have whatever you want. If I can afford it, it's yours.'

Irene put her arms around Boase's neck and kissed him.

'Archie Boase, I really love you. I really, really do.'

'Good. Well, on that note, I should be going. Now, have you locked up at the back? I'll just go and check, shall I?'

'You've already checked twice, Archie. It's all locked up.'

'I just worry about you, that's all. You're very precious to me.'

'I'm fine. Go home. I've got Topper here with me; he'll take care of me.'

Archie left by the front door. He waited on the step.

'Irene...'

'Yes, I know ... make sure I lock the door and draw the bolt across. Goodnight, Archie.'

'Goodnight, Irene. Pleasant dreams.'

Boase walked into his office at eight o'clock the next morning wondering how long it would be before he heard from Bartlett in response to his telegram. As he shut the door behind him he noticed some papers scattered on Bartlett's desk. As he walked across to look at them, the door opened and Bartlett stood there watching.

'Good morning, my boy. How are you?'

Boase spun round.

'Well, I'll be ... what on earth are you doing here, sir?'

'Hmmm. I've had better welcomes, I can safely say. Aren't you pleased to have me back, then?'

'Of course I am, sir. Did you get my telegram?'

'Yes, got it last night. That's why I came back – and, well, Mrs Bartlett was becoming restless. There was no point in her being away to recover if all she wanted to do was to come home because she was worried about the house and Irene.'

'The house was fine, sir. So was Irene.'

'Well. I knew you'd be keeping an eye on things – I told her so. But when I got the telegram we both agreed to come home. I couldn't leave you to deal with something that you were worried about. Now, send for some tea and let's talk.'

Bartlett regarded Boase over the top of his glasses.

'So what you're saying is that the old man killed himself? How? I don't understand. Explain your theory to me again, Boase.'

'Well, let's go back to the beginning. We thought that Clicker was murdered. Did we even once consider that he had done this to himself?'

'Why would we, Boase? But Greet is going to have a field day with this – he'll say we should have found the gun hanging in the tree.'

'Well, yes, but we'll have to cross that bridge when we come to it. The fact is that the gun was concealed because the tree was in leaf and it was only now that it could be seen. You never really believed that Edward James was the killer anyway, did you, sir?'

'I don't even know what I really thought, Boase. Tell me how this might have worked then. Greet is going to want to know all about this.'

'OK – forget the reason for his actions then and think about the practicalities. Clicker must have climbed the tree...'

'Stop there. He was an old man – could he have climbed that tree?'

'Well, apparently he was quite agile for his age – throwing himself around the circus ring. By all accounts he was quite energetic. So, yes, it was perfectly possible that he could have climbed that tree.'

'Go on, Boase.'

Bartlett was lighting his pipe and listening to the younger man. He didn't like what he was hearing. Not one bit.

'Well, say he climbs up the tree. All he then has to do, having attached the gun to the band, is to hitch it around the branch and climb back down holding it. Then, he puts the gun to his head, pulls the trigger and, as he falls, the gun is released from his grip and springs back on the band and disappears into the tree – completely concealed in the leaves. You've got to admit, sir, that's a strange sort of genius.'

'So, now you need to explain why he would have done such a thing. And I will need to put that theory to Greet.'

'Well – go back to the beginning, sir ... Molly was Clicker's daughter. Her mother, Margaret Field, had disappeared when she was pregnant with Molly, leaving Clicker bereft. She returned as Molly James and gave the impression that there was some hope that Clicker would see Margaret again – and that she was in a sanatorium in Switzerland, when in fact she had been dead for several years. Molly also gave Clicker the impression that there could be reconciliation if her mother could get well again – but that was going to cost money, money that the Jameses didn't have. So Clicker was paying rather large sums of money in the hope that Margaret would indeed get well and he would see her. But he must have smelled a rat whenever he mentioned travelling to Switzerland and Molly stopped him with some lame excuse every time.'

'Well, yes, you would think so – but she was his daughter and he loved her. Maybe he was afraid to upset the apple-cart.'

'Maybe so. Anyway, when Anne Warner discovered that Margaret Field was dead and that Clicker was being taken for a ride, she felt that she had to tell him – those two were very good friends, don't forget; they looked after one another. I think that Clicker may have thought there was nothing left for him – the love of his life was dead, and his own flesh and blood had been deceiving him.'

'Do you think that would be enough to tip him over the edge?'

'It's not impossible, is it?'

'I suppose not.'

'Well, then Molly found out that Anne had told Clicker about the con and killed her in revenge because she had dried up the money. That's one murder we were absolutely convinced of.'

'Well, what you say is not completely out of the way, I suppose. So, what do we do now? Greet has to know about this gun – and where you found it. We can't keep this from him – it's evidence.'

'Well, we'll have to go up and tell him straight away. Now.'

'He won't be in yet, I shouldn't think. You're right. We need to tell him what we've ... what you've discovered. Then it's over to him. If he wasn't so anxious to interfere in the beginning we wouldn't be in this mess, Boase.'

At half past ten, Bartlett and Boase returned to their shared office and sat down in their chairs. Bartlett fiddled with a pen on his desk. Boase repeatedly slid his top drawer open and closed. Open and closed.

'I cannot believe the blasted cheek of that man, Boase. I've had it with him. I have. How on *earth* does he think that this is my fault? Tell me how he could even think that? You know we got straight on with the investigation and then, and then ... when it wasn't happening quickly enough, he trampled on through with no regard for any of our previous efforts. He messed up the whole thing and now he's trying to disclaim responsibility. Well, I'm not taking that from him. No, I am not.'

'Well, sir, what can you do?'

'I'm going to go above him. I'm going to put in a complaint about him. He's severely lacking. He has no regard for police procedure. That man has been nothing but trouble since he came here. I've had enough, Boase. I either retire now, and let me tell you, that is very tempting at the moment but ... but that's what he wants. Yes, mark my words, he's doing this because he's not only a useless member of the force, he's also trying to get rid of me. He's been angling to push me out for a long time now. Well, actually – I don't feel inclined to give in to him. I'm taking this further, Boase. Yes. Wait and see – he's not going to get away with this.'

'Sir, can you really do that – to someone like him?'

'What? Of course I can. He's nobody. Got ideas above, he has. Well, I've put up with him and his ways for too long – and I've said nothing. You've witnessed that, Boase ... how even-tempered I've been with him, with ... with that excuse for a superintendent. Well, no more. It's come to an end. You heard the way he just spoke to us. I'm not taking that from him. I'll cook his goose.'

'Sir, you're going to create a lot of trouble here if you do this, aren't you?'

'I don't see why. The people at the top need to know that this man is completely incapable. Do you understand what he was implying when we were up there just now? He is directly holding me responsible for a man being wrongly executed. I'll have no more of it ... no more. I shall be writing a letter this evening.'

Chapter Sixteen

'Miss Bartlett, how lovely to see you. How is your dear mother – I haven't seen her for a little while now?'

Irene sat in the chair before a large mirror in the beauty salon, Chez Marguerite, and looked at herself and at her hair.

'What? Oh, I'm so sorry. Yes, my mother ... well, she's not too bad at the moment, thank you. She has her good days and bad days. Thank you for asking.'

Madame Marguerite surveyed Irene in the mirror as she removed the clasp that was keeping her long hair up in a loose bun. Irene sighed as her long hair cascaded around her shoulders.

'You have such beautiful hair, Miss Bartlett. Have you decided to have something a little different?'

'Yes. I have, Madame Marguerite. I want it all off.'

'*All off?*'

'Yes, I want something more modern. I'm a young woman, soon to be married and I find my hair now, well ... rather unbecoming. And childish.'

'But, Miss Bartlett, are you *absolutely* sure?'

'Yes. Absolutely. I want a Dutch bob. Look – like this.'

Irene opened her handbag and pulled a page

from a magazine. She held it up to Madame Marguerite. 'Look at this picture – it's Mary Thurman, the actress. She has her hair bobbed like this. Do you think I could have mine the same? It looks so pretty.'

Madame Marguerite regarded the article.

'Yes. I know Mary Thurman. It's a very pretty style, this is. But, Miss Bartlett, I don't want to turn away your custom...'

'It won't it suit me?' Irene looked dismayed.

Seeing her disappointment, Madame Marguerite patted her on the shoulder.

'Well, if you don't mind my saying so – you do have a look of Miss Thurman. So young and elegant. Yes, why not? If that's what you want.'

Irene turned the key in the front door and went into the hall.

'Irene is that you, dear?'

'Yes, Mum. I'm just going upstairs to change my shoes. I won't be a moment.'

Irene hung her coat on the stand and, patting Topper on the head as he jumped up at her, went upstairs. She went into her bedroom and rushed to the mirror. Slowly she removed her hat. What was Archie going to say? She went back down the stairs and into the kitchen.

'Hello, Mum. Everything all right?'

Caroline Bartlett turned as her daughter entered the room.

'Irene! Oh, my. What *have* you done to your beautiful hair?'

'Don't you like it, Mum?'

'Well, it's just a bit of a shock, dear. I've only

ever seen you with long hair since you were a little girl.'

'But I'm not a little girl any more, Mum – I'll be getting married soon. A married woman needs to look grown-up.'

'Yes, dear – I know, you're right. And I think it looks lovely, very elegant. Yes, I like it very much.'

A delighted bark from Topper announced the arrival of George Bartlett. Irene went out into the hall to meet him.

'Hello, Dad. Everything all right?'

Bartlett looked at his daughter and smiled.

'You've done something ... to your hair, haven't you?'

'Is it OK, Dad?'

'Turn round. Well, I think that looks very nice. Yes, very nice indeed. Look, Princess, Irene's been to the hairdresser's – what do you think about her new hair?'

'An' don't come back!'

David Rowe slammed shut the door of the Seven Stars' public bar. He turned to Bessie Penhaligon.

'Bessie, I don't want that man coming in 'ere no more. If 'e turns up, you just send for me. Understand? The man's a menace. I know 'e's 'igh up in the local force but policeman or no, I won't let 'im in 'ere again if 'e can't hold 'is drink. I've got customers complaining about 'im all the time. 'E's gone too far with me. My patience 'as run out. Every time I open up, there 'e is, on the step. Why doesn't 'e drink somewhere else?'

David Rowe had been the landlord of the Seven Stars for many years. Everyone thought him a rather funny little man – but very amenable. At only five feet tall he had negotiated the height of the bar for his first year and then given in and had a step built in behind it, from end to end. Everyone was amused to see him walk along behind the bar and then step down like a small child. Despite this, he took no trouble from anyone and coped admirably even when throwing out men much larger than himself.

Bessie wiped the bar with a cloth then began to empty the ashtrays.

'Well, 'e'll 'ave to find somewhere else to drink now – seein' as you've barred 'im.'

'Yes, indeed, 'e will. I don't suppose it'll be long before 'e's barred from everywhere else too. I have run this public house for a very long time – and it has a good reputation. I don't want people like that ruining it. Mr Hingston was in 'ere last night and said he wasn't going to come back – 'e felt so uncomfortable. 'e's a very good customer – and, what's more, 'e always recommends this place to people who want a drink or people who want somewhere to stay. 'e meets plenty of them on that boat of 'is and I think I've probably done quite well on the back of 'is recommendations. I don't want to start upsetting people like him. He told me that that man was down on the Prince of Wales Pier two nights in a row, causing trouble. Apparently 'e'd bin drinking – 'eavily. Hingston was there with some of the other boatmen, just 'avin' a yarn ... before they knew what was 'appening they 'eard a splash and there 'e was – in the sea. Luckily they were quick an' dragged un out.'

'Well, you know I've known James Hingston for years – 'e still lives right by me. I'll look in on 'im later and tell 'im you've dealt with that horrible man.'

'If you wouldn't mind. I like the man, Hingston – he's a real gentleman. This place could do with a few more like 'im.'

'Well, I don't understand it, Mr Rowe, really I don't. I'm so pleased you threw 'im out of 'ere. 'E used to be a well-respected man in the town. Now look what 'e's come to, and what with him so high up in the police.'

'Yes, quite. How the mighty have fallen. It don't take much to fall to nothing these days, Bessie – the smallest thing can tip a man over the edge. And, although I myself am in the business of providing good-quality liquor to the public, I do 'ave to say that a man – or a woman mind, I do not discriminate in this – with too much drink in is a terrible thing to behold. Shows a terrible lack of self-control. Look at your Edward.'

'Oh ... do I 'ave to? – that's the last thing I want to look at after a night in 'ere, Mr Rowe.' Bessie Penhaligon let out a shrill peal of laughter that echoed around the bar.

'I'm only saying, Bessie, that 'usband of yours, well, I've known 'im for many years, as you are aware, and a nicer young man I could not 'ave wished to meet. Then ... what did 'e do? Yes, 'e turned to drink – right before your very eyes. Terrible, terrible tragedy.'

'But you've 'elped me keep 'im on the straight an' narrow, Mr Rowe. You've been a life-saver to me, you really 'ave.'

David Rowe patted Bessie on the hand and the pair began to reminisce about the terrible night that Bessie had just left her shift in the Seven Stars. David, always a gentleman, had offered to walk her home – she and Edward had couple of rented rooms at the top of High Street. As they were halfway up the hill, Bessie had spotted her husband coming down, arm in arm with a dreadful-looking woman. She'd nudged David and they'd stepped back into the shadows, waiting for the other pair to pass. Bessie had watched as her husband lit two cigarettes and handed one to the woman, who was giggling and stumbling on her too-high heels. She'd draped her arms around Edward and he pulled a bottle from his pocket and held it, first to her lips and then to his. They had reached May's Haberdashers and were standing outside, the woman leaning against the window, when Edward grabbed her waist and pulled her into the shop doorway.

Bessie had started to cry. Seeing her distress, David Rowe could take no more. He'd walked into the doorway and dragged the woman away, pushing her aside. When Edward saw David coming at him he had put up his fists in defence, but David had quickly slapped the taller man's face with his left hand, disorientating him, then swung at him with the right.

David's blow had launched Edward Penhaligon straight through the large sheet of glass which formed the main part of the shop window. The next morning Edward had still been unconscious, and the shopkeeper had found him lying inside the shop amongst the haberdashery and fancy goods.

'Yes – 'e went wrong all because of drink. But I 'ope things are settling a bit for you now, Bessie.'

Bessie said no more but carried on quietly cleaning up.

George Bartlett sat on a bench in his garden. Topper lay at his feet.

'Dad ... Dad – would you like a cup of tea?'

Irene called to her father through the open kitchen window.

'I'd rather have one of my beers, if it's all the same to you, Irene.'

'That's fine, Dad. No problem, wait a minute.'

Irene opened a bottle of Leonard's London Beer and poured it into a glass for her father. Grabbing his newspaper from a small table in the hall, she went out into the garden.

'Here you are, Dad. Are you sure you're all right?'

'Yes. I'm fine, Irene. Stop worrying.'

Caroline stood up from her place on the bench next to her husband.

'I'll just fetch my pills, I don't want to forget them again.'

'No, Princess. You don't. Here, Irene. Why don't you take the weight off for a minute or two?'

'Well, OK – just for a minute then. Are you happy now that your awful boss has been moved on, Dad? He was making you really unhappy, wasn't he?'

'Well, yes, he was. I found him to be very unfair – and slack, Irene. If you can't give a job your all then, well, really you may as well not bother.'

'So, has he gone for good then, Dad?'

'Well, I think so. Apparently he didn't have a very good record where he was before. Looks like he only got on because it was his turn ... not because he was any good at his job. I don't know how he got away with it for so long. He's in his forties now, I think – he'll probably be given another job elsewhere. When's that prospective son-in-law of mine expected to turn up? If he doesn't get a move on, I'll have drunk all the beer.'

'He'll be here soon, Dad. We're going to the pictures. There's a film with Mary Thurman – she's the one with hair like mine – well, I should say I copied her.'

'That's nice, dear.'

At that, Topper bounded across the garden in front of Boase who came out onto the lawn clutching a bottle of Leonard's.

'Hello, all.'

Bartlett looked up.

'Didn't take you long to sniff out my beer.'

'Mrs Bartlett gave it to me when I arrived. Is that OK?' Bartlett chuckled.

'Of course it is, my boy. I'm happy to share my beer with you any time – and I'm exceedingly happy that you appear to have grown to appreciate it. Everything all right with you, Boase?'

Boase had seen Irene sitting on the bench next to her father. He stared at her. Next he walked around the back of the bench. He stared again. She turned around.

'Archie ... what's wrong?'

'Irene, you know what's wrong.' Boase touched Irene's hair with his fingertips. 'What have you

213

done to your lovely hair? You didn't say you were going to do this.'

'Don't you like it, Archie?'

'Well, you could have said something before you did it.'

'I'm sorry, Archie – I didn't think.'

'Well, it's done now.'

Irene ran across the lawn and back into the house. Bartlett glanced at Boase.

'Don't you think you should go after her? You've upset her there, Boase.'

'No ... I should probably leave her. I can't believe she did that to her hair. I mean – why would she do that? Her hair was beautiful.'

'Well, I can't disagree, but the one thing you're overlooking, my boy – and if you don't mind my saying so, is that it *is* her hair. She can do whatever she likes with it.'

Boase pursued this no further. 'Sir, did you hear what happened in the Seven Stars last night?'

'No – what's that, then?'

'Apparently, Superintendent Greet was in there last night...'

'Oh? Really? Didn't know he was a drinker.'

'Well, he was in there until he got thrown out.'

Bartlett put down his glass.

'Thrown out? Thrown out for what?'

'Apparently he was drunk, blind drunk – everyone saw what happened.'

'Why is he behaving like that?'

'Well, sir – I don't know how to say this ... people are saying it's because he's lost his job.'

'Oh – and they think that's because of me? Well, he had every opportunity to work with me when

214

he pitched up there and he wasted it. He's upset everyone in that station, no one likes him and no one can work with him. And I know we've all tried. He isn't thorough in his work and he blames everyone else for his own shortcomings. He's not a nice person to know. So, I'm sorry and all that, but something needed to be said and, well, if his superiors deemed that he should no longer be allowed to continue in that particular position then that is not down to me.'

'George!'

Caroline had crossed the lawn from the house just in time to hear this outburst from her husband. She sat down next to him.

'I hardly recognise you when you say things like that, George. Don't be like that, dear. So, what time are you and Irene going out, Archie?'

Boase looked at his watch.

'Well, we really should be going now.'

'Well, Irene is in the kitchen – she's a little upset about you not liking her hair.'

Boase walked into the house.

'Is it OK to leave now, Irene?'

'Of course it is, Archie. I've been really looking forward to this. Finish your beer and we can go.'

Irene waved at her parents from the kitchen door and she and Boase left.

In the garden, Caroline looked at her husband.

'George – you can't afford to get so worked up about things, dear.'

'I know, Princess. I thought when Greet was put out that things would be better. Look, he's still causing trouble. No wonder he hasn't got a wife –

shouldn't think anyone would take him on.'

'Stop it now, dear. Come on, finish your beer. Have a look at your paper. Forget about work for one night.'

Bartlett shook open the newspaper and, pulling his reading spectacles from his top pocket, settled down in the garden to read.

Irene slipped her arm through Boase's as they walked down Killigrew. He didn't speak.

She squeezed his arm and looked up at him. Still nothing.

'Archie. Don't be angry with me. I didn't cut my hair to upset you.'

'Well, you may as well have.'

Irene stopped walking and looked up at her fiancé.

'Archie – you really *are* behaving like an idiot. This is nothing. Why shouldn't I be able to cut my hair if I like? It's my hair and I shall do as I please with it.'

'Well, you always do as you please, don't you, Irene? Anything you want, you get. You're such a spoilt little girl.'

'Archie Boase! Take that back immediately. What a horrible thing to say.'

'No, actually, Irene, I'm not going to take it back. I mean every word of it.'

'Well, if you don't take it back, you can go on your own.'

'There you go again – being childish.'

'Well you're not exactly being an adult, are you?'

'Not being an adult? Not being an adult? How

216

dare you, Irene Bartlett. You have no idea of anything in your silly, sheltered little life, have you? When I was in France I saw things that would make your stomach turn over. Things that I can never forget seeing and hearing. All those young men, dying in pain, in agony, calling for their mothers. You have no idea of life, Irene. No idea of this world at all. Young men – no, boys – who will never come home again to England, to Cornwall. They will never hold the women of their dreams close to them all night and wake up with them in the morning–'

'Archie Boase, that's disgusting talk. I'm ashamed of you.'

Irene dealt Boase a sharp blow across the side of his face. He drew back in surprise.

'I don't care if I never see you again. I don't know how I ever got involved with you. You're a horrible person and I'm just glad I found out about you before it was too late.'

Holding back the tears which were now pricking her face, she turned and walked back up Killigrew and she was gone. Boase put his hand to his face. It was still stinging, so sharp was the blow.

Chapter Seventeen

Over the coming days, Bartlett and Boase made out their reports on the new and recent findings at Hunter's Path and this was investigated with gravity. Greet's replacement was anxiously being awaited.

Bernard Pellow sat on the steps of the Passmore Edwards Free Library on the Moor. He pulled a copy of the *Falmouth Packet* from his delivery bag and looked at the front page. As he began to read, Michael Crago walked past, pushing his bicycle.

'Come on, Pellow – I don't pay you to deliver my papers and then expect to see you sitting on the steps reading them. Get on.'

'I'm sorry, Michael – didn't expect to see you walking past.'

'Obviously.'

Bernard folded up the paper and returned it to his bag. He stood up, unsteadily on his feet.

'You all right, Bernard?'

Michael Crago put out his hand for support.

'Yes, thanks, Michael – it's just these blasted dizzy turns. I thought I'd be feeling better now but I'm not. Can't get rid of the sound of the guns. What is the point of war? Why did we all have to go through that?'

'I don't know the answer to that, my friend.

What I do know is that I'm glad you were with me in France. I couldn't have got through without you. You really need to see your doctor again about all these turns you keep having. I'm sure there must be something he can do for you. Now, how much more have you got in that bag? Let's have a look. Oh, you've almost finished. Look – why don't I take these few and finish up for you?'

'Because you're my boss, Michael.'

'You were my boss in France, Bernard – you helped me.'

Bernard handed over the bag containing the newspapers and Michael took it, attaching it to the back of his bicycle.

'I won't ever forget what you did for me over there, Bernard. Never. Now, why don't you finish for the day – go home and see how your mother is. Give her my best, won't you?'

'I will. Thank you, Michael.'

Michael pushed off on his bicycle, only turning once to call out.

'Tell her not to forget that pasty she promised me!'

Bernard smiled and thought how lucky he was to have a good friend like Michael – and how grateful he was for him giving him a job in his newsagent's shop.

Michael Crago delivered the last few newspapers, all but two. They were out of his way a little and so he had left them until last. He walked along Penwerris Terrace, climbing the high pavement halfway along and lifting up his bicycle.

As he reached the first of his two customers' houses, Number Ten, he laid his bicycle against the front wall and walked through the front garden gate. He checked the name pencilled on the top of the newspaper and realised that this was an overdue bill. He checked the name again ... he thought so. *Superintendent Greet. It wasn't like him to leave his bill to mount up. Maybe with all that business at the police station, he had forgotten.* Michael hoped that the superintendent hadn't already left town without paying him. He'd heard what the police were like sometimes – not always whiter than white.

He knocked at the front door and waited. He turned to look out across the harbour, watching the gulls circling over the small boats. He waited a little longer then decided that the superintendent must be out. He drew a piece of paper from his jacket pocket together with a small pencil and began to write a hasty note detailing the outstanding debt. As he stood on the doorstep, writing, a woman opened the front door of the house next but one and called to him.

'Hey, mister.'

Michael turned to see who was calling to him.

'Yes, madam. What is it?'

'That man. The policeman 'oo lives there...'

'Yes, madam. What about him?'

'Well, 'e's disappeared. No one 'as seen 'im since the night 'e was thrown out the Seven Stars. You can knock as loud as you like – 'e's not there. We always saw 'im goin' back and forth – but no ... no sight nor sound. So – if it's money you're after, don't bother. He's vanished, I tell 'e.'

'Well, thank you for that, madam. I bid you good morning.'

The neighbour disappeared and Michael folded the piece of paper into two. He leaned forward in order to post the note through the letterbox – just in case Superintendent Greet had not absconded and was, indeed, still living at this address.

As Michael Crago pushed open the small letter box, his eyes were drawn to the back of the hall. He closed the letter box quickly and it snapped shut, almost trapping his fingers. He turned away from the front door, unsure of what he had seen. He regarded the sea and the harbour, took a deep breath and, after this respite, turned to look through the tiny letter box again. Surely this time he would see something else?

No. Everything was exactly the same as the first time he had looked. He dropped the note he had just written and ran back down the garden path. Grabbing his bicycle, he mounted it and cycled off at top speed on the raised pavement, heading towards town.

Reaching the police station, Michael Crago ran inside and up to the desk. He addressed the sergeant.

'I want to see Inspector Bartlett – please, quickly.'

The desk sergeant looked at him.

'Well, I really think you should calm down a little, Mr Crago. What's the hurry?'

'I just need to see him – or Archie Boase. Quickly, please. It's so urgent.'

'Wait 'ere.'

The sergeant knocked on Bartlett and Boase's

door and walked in.

'I'm so sorry to disturb you both – Mr Crago's outside. You know – the newsagent chappie. Says 'e 'as to see you urgently.'

Bartlett removed his reading spectacles and looked up.

'Well, send him in.'

Michael Crago entered the office.

'Good morning, Inspector Bartlett. Hello, Archie.'

'What's happened, Michael? You look like you've seen a ghost.'

Bartlett offered the man a chair and he sat down.

'Inspector Bartlett, I think something terrible has happened. You need to come with me, at once.'

At this, Michael Crago began to shake uncontrollably.

'Boase, fetch him some tea.'

'No, Inspector. You must listen and then we must leave immediately.'

Bartlett sat back in his chair and waited patiently. He didn't much like the theatrical dimension now being lent to this conversation.

Within fifteen minutes, a car carrying Bartlett, Boase, Coad and Michael Crago had stopped outside number ten, Penwerris Terrace. Boase looked through the letter box. 'He's right, sir – he's in there.'

Boase, with the help of Coad, forced open the front door and they both ran into the hall. Bartlett followed. As he reached the staircase, he looked down to see Superintendent Bertram Greet lying on the floor. Next to his outstretched hand was a pill bottle.

'How long do you think he's been here, sir?'

'I have no idea, Boase. We need to find out if he did this to himself, though.'

'He must have, sir. You don't suspect foul play here, do you?'

'Not necessarily – but we have to look at every possibility, you know that, Boase. See to it that this is sorted out here, will you?'

Bartlett walked back through the hall and out into the sunshine. He sat on the wall. Michael Crago came and sat next him.

'Did he kill himself, Inspector Bartlett?'

'Well, I can't actually discuss that with you, Michael. Why don't you get along now? Thank you for letting us know about ... this. Will you be all right?'

'Yes, of course I will. Thank you. I'll be getting along then. Goodbye, Inspector Bartlett.'

'Goodbye, Michael.'

Boase came back out of the house.

'You OK, sir?'

'Yes. Yes, Boase. What did he want to do a damn fool thing like that for? What an idiot.'

'You mustn't blame yourself, sir.'

'What? I'm not blaming myself, Boase. Why should I? I'm just saying the man was an idiot. That's all.'

Boase turned away from Bartlett momentarily and gathered his thoughts. He turned back again.

'Sir, if you don't mind me saying – I think you need to put all this behind you now. I know he made things difficult for you.'

'Difficult? Difficult doesn't cover it, Boase. That man in there...'

'Sir! That man, in there, is lying dead. Now that's a terrible thing for anyone, especially if he has done this to himself, which looks likely. Surely now you can find some compassion? You really need to stop this now, sir – for your own sanity ... and dignity.'

At this, George Bartlett put his head in his hands and wept.

Boase knelt down next to Bartlett.

'Sir? Sir ... what on earth has happened? Talk to me, sir.'

'Boase – look what a terrible person I'm turning into. That man is lying in there, dead – and all because of me. Because I couldn't be tolerant. Now look at the trouble I've caused. And you're right, even now I'm showing no compassion. What would Caroline say? She'd be so ashamed of me.'

'Well, you've been under a lot of strain recently, sir. You know that. You probably haven't been able to look at things with a clear mind. Don't let it get you down – you'll drive yourself mad with it all. You really need a rest – you shouldn't have come back early from Perranporth.'

'Well, I had to. I had work to do.'

'I know, sir. But I can see what a strain this case has put on you – you're doing too much.'

Bartlett stood up and walked back to the car.

Where should he go from here? He felt at such a low point in his life now.

'What's the verdict then, sir?'

224

'It's definitely suicide, Boase – nothing fishy happened. That's for certain. Greet killed himself when he was not in his right mind due to nervous exhaustion and stress.'

'So, what happens now?'

'Well, nothing. His family is coming down to take his body back to ... I don't know. Where is he from, Boase?'

'Manchester, I think, sir.'

'Yes, that's right, Manchester, I knew it was a long way away – yes, I remember him telling me. They're expected later today. There's his widow – I understand they were estranged at the time of his death – and two sons. I'm sorry it's all ended like this, Boase. I know I didn't see eye to eye with Greet about – well, really about anything, his methods or ideas about policing. I didn't even like the man but, still, this is a bad business.'

'If we're being honest, sir, no one saw eye to eye with him. He was very difficult to get along with.'

'Yes, he was that.'

Bartlett looked at Boase.

'Why are you looking at me, sir? Have I got food on my mouth?'

Boase wiped his mouth with the back of his hand.

'No, my boy. I was rather wondering what you're going to do about Irene. She came home the last time she was with you vowing never to speak to you again. I thought you two had big plans. Are you just going to leave things as they are?'

'I don't know, sir. I haven't decided.'

'You haven't decided – that's very childish behaviour, if you ask me. You two were very serious about each other, engaged to be married. Now you stand there and say you haven't decided what to do. Well, I wouldn't hang about if I were you – if you want to go back to how you were, you need to get a move on. You know how single-minded Irene can be. Downright stubborn, in fact.'

Boase looked at Bartlett and wondered where on earth Irene's stubbornness could have come from. Stubborn? George Bartlett had invented stubborn.

'Well, what can I do, sir? I really upset her and she's saying she doesn't want to see me again.'

'Just go and see her. Maybe don't tell her you're coming, just turn up one evening and take her out for a walk or something. I don't know but you two need to talk. You surely can't throw everything away just on one quarrel.'

'I suppose I have been a bit stupid, haven't I? But that business with her hair – it just really upset me.'

'Well, you'll never control Irene. You must already know that – yes, she's her own woman and I'm very proud of her for that. She's honest, she speaks her mind and she's loyal. So, if you can't handle her then…'

'Who says I can't handle her? I'll be round at six – don't tell her I'm coming.'

Bartlett sat back in his chair and grinned. He'd get this patched up yet.

At half past one, Ernest Penhaligon knocked on the door of Bartlett's office and entered. Bartlett looked up.

'What is it, Penhaligon?'

'Sir, Superintendent Greet's family have just arrived. They want to speak to you.'

'Tell them to wait a moment.'

He turned to Boase.

'Blast them. What do they want *me* for?'

Boase stood up behind his desk.

'I don't know, sir, but I'm with you, whatever it is. Have they come to cause trouble?'

'Don't see why. Show them in here, Boase.'

Bartlett and Boase introduced themselves to Superintendent Greet's family. His widow was accompanied by her two sons, Albert and George. The younger, George, Bartlett couldn't help noticing, looked exactly like his father and this unnerved him. This particular Greet spoke first.

'Inspector Bartlett. I wanted you to know how dismayed we are at your treatment of our father, your superior. I know I speak for all three of us when I say that my father found you extremely difficult to work with, insolent and downright awkward. I understand that you made a very serious accusation against my father, in fact several accusations, and I wish you to know that I am lodging a formal counter-complaint against you. My father found you wanting in every respect and I, we, hold you entirely responsible, through your recent actions, for the fate that befell him.'

Bartlett stood up from his seat.

'Now you look here...'

The elder Greet, who had been standing next to his brother and behind their mother, stepped forward.

'There is nothing more to say on this matter, Inspector Bartlett. Out of courtesy we are advising you of the actions we will be taking against you. There is nothing further to discuss. I bid you good day.'

The widow, who had not spoken a word, looked up as her elder son offered his hand to her and she rose from the chair she had occupied during this brief meeting. Boase held the door open for the pair and, as the last of the three left the office, Boase slammed it firmly shut.

Archie Boase, wearing his best navy blue suit, walked in the direction of Penmere Hill and the Bartletts' house. As he turned at the top of the hill, he paused, brushed his jacket and adjusted his cuffs. He walked another fifty yards then stopped in his tracks at the scene which met him. Coming up the hill was Irene Bartlett with a man. Her arm was through his and he appeared to Boase to be more than attentive. They were too busy to have seen him and didn't avert their gaze on each other until Boase was standing feet in front of them. Irene blushed slightly.

'Archie! What are *you* doing here?'

'Well, I *was* coming to see you, Irene. But it looks like you're busy.'

Boase stared hard at the man.

'Archie, this is Gerald Tregidgo; we were at school together. We're just going to the pictures.'

'I thought you liked *me* taking you to the pictures?'

'But we didn't go and I want to go now. Gerald offered and I said yes. Is there a problem?'

'I'd say so. Irene, I think you should tell Gerald to run along home.'

'No, I won't.'

At this, Gerald stepped forward and, being of a similar height, stared Boase in the eyes.

'Why don't you leave Irene alone. You've already upset her enough, from what I've heard.'

'So we have no private business either, Irene?'

Gerald put his hand on Boase's sleeve and Boase pushed him away.

'Don't you lay a hand on me – or my girl.'

'She's not your girl.'

Their voices were becoming louder now and Irene stepped away from the two men. Gerald tried to push Boase and, now beyond anger and all reason, Boase landed a punch straight to the other man's jaw. Irene, horrified, drew back further. Gerald, put his hand to his lip and, on seeing a bright red streak of blood, came back at Boase and threw a punch straight to his stomach. The pair wrestled each other to the ground as Irene ran back to the house to fetch her father. By the time Bartlett had come the short distance up the hill, Gerald was lying on the ground, not moving and Boase was standing over him. Bartlett knelt down on the ground and inspected the casualty.

'Boase, what are you playing at? Why did you do this?'

Gerald was now moaning and had his hand clasped to his head. Irene pushed Boase in the chest and he winced.

'Archie – how could you do this to my friend?'

'I thought *I* was your friend, Irene – you don't need him.'

229

'He's just a friend and I thought I made it plain to you before that I won't be upset by you. And all this just because I cut my hair. Archibald Boase – you don't own me!'

At this, Irene marched off back down Penmere Hill and into the house.

'Help me to get him up, Boase. I hope for your sake he doesn't make a complaint.'

Together, they managed to lift Gerald to his feet.

'We'll have to take him to our house and try to clean him up a bit – you're such an idiot, Boase!'

'Why didn't you tell Irene to expect me?'

'I seem to remember you telling me not to.'

Gerald Tregidgo lay on the couch in the Bartlett parlour. Irene made him some tea. She sat with him and held the teacup to his mouth. She looked up at Boase.

'Archie, I think you should leave now. You've caused enough trouble.'

Bartlett followed Boase to the front door.

'Well, that didn't have the desired effect, did it? She's with him and you're out on your elbow. You're such a fool, Boase. Get off home and hope no one finds out about all this.'

Boase walked slowly back up Penmere Hill. His ribs were hurting and the stitching was coming apart on his best blue suit. He stopped at the top of the road and sat on a wall. He'd only worn the suit for Irene. She always said how handsome he looked when he wore it. Now it was ruined and so was his life with her. What on *earth* had he been thinking? Scrapping in the road like that – and in front of the love of his life? This could never be put right. Boase sat with his head in his hands and a tear rolled down his cheek as he thought about what he'd now probably lost for good. For ever. The one thing he'd wanted for so long.

Three long days passed and Boase had heard nothing from Irene. Worse, to his mind, Bartlett had not spoken about her or the incident in Penmere Hill – other than to say the following morning that he thought Boase to be a fool to risk so much – his future happiness with his wife and possibly even his job and his reputation. To be fair, Bartlett had not held it against Boase once he had said what he needed to say and the subject wasn't mentioned again. Bartlett had been young once and, while probably not so hot-headed as Boase, he could understand why his colleague had got so fired up when he saw Irene with another man, albeit it a friend.

So, for three days, the subject remained closed. On the fourth day, Bartlett surveyed Boase from his desk. He held a piece of paper aloft.

'You got lucky, Boase. You got very lucky. Gerald Tregidgo – he put in a formal complaint against you but it says here that he retracted it later.'

'Well, he's got a blasted cheek if you ask me, sir. Making a complaint when he had stolen my fiancée right from under my nose.'

'Boase, I think you should count yourself very lucky. You've got away with it this time – and I would say that this retraction has more than a little to do with Irene. And, you shouldn't be surprised at her actions ... stepping out with Gerald. He's just an old friend of hers but, whoever he is, you had no right to do what you did. Anyway, we should drop it now. You're an idiot – let's leave it at that, shall we?'

'He had it coming...'

'Boase!'

Bartlett had had enough and Boase realised it was time to stop.

Chapter Eighteen

Constable Ernest Penhaligon spat hard on his boots and polished them vigorously. Boase watched him as he stood in the doorway of the makeshift kitchen and boot room. He waved a piece of fruit cake in Penhaligon's direction.

'I've got some more of this, if you want a piece, Penhaligon?'

'No thanks. I'm going to make some tea now – all this business is proper drying me out.'

'Why are you being so diligent over your boots anyway? You don't usually bother.'

'Well, actually, I consider my boots to be the most highly polished boots in this station and, as you already know, we're meeting the new superintendent this morning.'

'That's today?!'

'Yes.'

'Crikey – I thought it was tomorrow.'

'No. He's coming today at one o'clock.'

Boase walked swiftly back to his office and stood in front of George Bartlett's desk. Bartlett looked up.

'Yes? Why are you standing there staring at me, Boase?'

'Did you know it was today, sir?'

'Did I know what was today?'

'The new Superintendent is coming here – today.'

'Today? No, I most certainly did not. And how do you know?'

'Penhaligon told me.'

'And how does Penhaligon know before us?'

'I dunno, sir.'

'Right, well we'd better get some sort of order in here – the place is a mess. When is he arriving?'

'At one, sir.'

'Right, well that only gives us two hours – go round and make sure everything looks all right, will you, Boase? Don't take any nonsense from anyone. We don't want to get off on the wrong foot with this one if we can help it. Now's our chance to make this station a better place for everyone to work in – especially us.'

Superintendent James Bolton stood in front of his police officers. He walked up and down the line and studied them hard. He stopped in front of Constable Eddy and, with one hand, swiftly brushed across the officer's shoulder. The two men looked at each other and Bolton moved on.

'All I have to say to you gentlemen is this – if you fall in with me, then I'll fall in with you. I know my predecessor was not an easy man to get

233

along with and you didn't see much of him, but I think you will find me different. In the first place, my door is always open to you. I will back each and every one of you – always. But, if one of you is found to cross me and not be backing me in return, and in my efforts to run this station then, well, then things will begin to look a little different. So, what I'm saying is that I'm counting on you and you're counting on me. We need to make this work – just remember that there are enough people at the top waiting to knock us down without us doing it to each other here in Falmouth. I hope I've made myself clear to you.'

The group was dismissed and went about their business. Bartlett and Boase went into their office.

'Well, what do you make of him, sir?'

'Well, I'm not sure – he's a bit different from Greet, don't you think?'

'Yes, I think so. We might find him a bit easier to get along with – hopefully.'

'Yes, hopefully.'

A knock at the door was followed by the desk sergeant's head appearing round it.

'Excuse me, Inspector Bartlett, Superintendent Bolton would like to see you, now, please.'

'Righto – I'm coming.'

Bartlett stood up and brushed off his jacket. He looked at Boase.

'Wonder what he wants me for?'

'Only one way to find out, sir.'

Bartlett left and went upstairs.

'Come in, George. Can I call you George – is that all right?'

'Well, that's my name, sir. Yes, of course you can.'

'Good. Sit down, George.'

'Why did you want to see me, sir?'

'I wanted, firstly, to say hello to you away from everyone else – I've heard good things about you, George, here at Falmouth and in London and I don't want to lose you.'

'Well I don't think you'll be losing me quite yet, sir.'

'George – this is where we may have a problem.'

'Oh?'

'Yes. Superintendent Greet's family – they were here before. They told you they were going to put in a high-level complaint against you, didn't they?'

'Yes. Yes, they did. Why? What's happened?'

'Well, they've gone ahead with their threat. They've complained and in no small way.'

'Oh, no.'

Bartlett was visibly shocked.

'George, can I get you something? I'll send for some tea – you look a little unwell.'

Bolton went quickly to the door and, leaning over the stair rail, called down to Penhaligon in the lobby.

'Penhaligon, bring some tea for Inspector Bartlett, will you? Be quick.'

The tea, fortuitously having been already freshly brewed, was brought into the superintendent's office and Bartlett gratefully accepted it.

'Bit better now, George?'

'Yes. I'm all right, sir. Don't worry – it's been a hard couple of weeks. I'm fine now. Thank you.'

'Look, I want to help you here, George. This isn't going to be easy. I had no idea how influential Greet's family actually are.'

'What do you mean, sir?'

'It seems that it's a family occupation – not just Greet but several of his family are in the force, a couple of them quite high up, apparently. So that will make it difficult for you – for us.'

'How? What will be difficult?'

'They want you gone, George. Out of the force. I want you to stay – you're a good policeman and you've got more left in you yet. I need you here. But they want you finished.'

George Bartlett sat in his armchair in the parlour. Caroline and Irene listened to the story he relayed.

'George, dear. What does this *mean?*'

'It means they want me out, Princess. And it looks like they'll get their way.'

'Dad!'

'It's all right, Irene. It's probably coming time I thought about finishing now. I *would* have liked to do it in my own time – on my terms.'

'But, dear, it looks like your new boss is fighting in your corner.'

'Yes, he is – I wish he could have come to us a long time ago. Nevertheless, I don't see what he can do to help. I haven't been suspended but, well, if they tell me to go, then I have to go.'

Topper suddenly stood up from his place next to Bartlett's chair and walked into the hall, his tail wagging. He let out two small barks. Caroline got up and followed the dog into the hall. A familiar silhouette appeared in the glass panes of the front door. Caroline went across the hall and opened it.

'Oh, hello, Archie. How are you?'

'I'm very well, thank you – I was wondering if Irene was in?'

'Yes, yes, she is. Umm – would you like to come in?' Boase, clutching an extremely large bouquet of flowers stepped across the threshold.

'Irene ... Archie's come to see you.'

Irene looked at her father and he winked at her.

'Go and see what he wants.'

Irene went out into the hall. Boase handed her the flowers and as she took them, he touched her hand. She drew it away quickly. Bartlett called to them.

'Why don't you two go and sit in the garden? I expect you want to talk.'

The couple went out through the back door and into the garden.

'Shall we sit on the seat, Irene? I'd like to talk to you.'

'Do you think they'll be all right, George – after their little falling out?'

'I'm sure they will. They think very highly of each other – no doubt about that. We had a few little rows before we were married, if my memory serves me right?'

'Yes, dear, we did. But that business the other evening – and the fight ... well, we never let things get that bad, did we?'

'No, we didn't – but just don't interfere. They're old enough to know what they're doing. They don't need intervention from us.'

'If you say so, dear.'

Caroline moved across to the window and looked out into the garden.

'Sit down, Princess – they'll see you. I said leave them to it.'

'Very well, dear. Whatever you say.'

'Irene – I've been such an idiot. Can you forgive me? I'm so sorry.'

'What you did, Archibald Boase, what you did was unforgivable. In the first place, to think that I could not meet with an old friend, and in the second place, well, to cause so much trouble and to hurt another person like that...'

'You hurt me, Irene. I thought you were my girl.'

'I was. But you ruined that, Archie Boase. You're a horrible, jealous, violent man. Now please go. I don't want to see you again.'

'Irene, please, dearest Irene. Please don't say such things. I love you with all my heart. For ever. Please don't push me away. Please don't. How can I say how sorry I am? What do you want me to do? I'll do anything to show you how much you mean to me.'

Boase took Irene's hand in his. She tried to pull away but he held her small hand firmly and he kissed it.

'Irene, my darling Irene. Please don't send me away like this.'

'Archie. Please go. I *can't* forgive you. I don't

238

like what I saw in you.'

Irene ran across the lawn, into the house and upstairs to her room. Bartlett stood up from his chair and ran to the door.

'George, leave her alone. She'll tell us when she's ready.'

Bartlett went to the back door and saw Boase slumped on the garden seat.

'George, leave them both, please. You were right – let them deal with it – *we* never wanted people interfering.'

'But what on earth has she said to him?'

'She'll tell us when she needs to.'

Bartlett turned and looked again into the garden. The seat was empty.

'It's at half past eight, Boase.'

'What is, sir? What's at half past eight?'

'You just this minute asked me what time is my meeting with Bolton.'

'Oh, sir. I'm so sorry – yes I did, didn't I? I feel a little out of sorts this morning. I apologise.'

'Irene?'

Boase fiddled with a pencil, turning it over and over in his hands. His head was down.

'Boase – don't put your head down. Face up to what's happening like a man.'

'But I don't know what's happening, sir. Irene doesn't want me and I don't know what I can do about it. She's a very single-minded girl, as well you know.'

'Yes, yes she is, my boy. She made it quite plain to her mother and me that she wanted nothing more to do with you – and that's her decision to make, but...'

'But what, sir?' Boase looked up hopefully.

'Well, are you going to let her go, or are you going to fight for her? And I do not mean fight like the other night – that's what caused this mess in the first place.'

'Is there any point in fighting? She's made up her mind about me now.'

'Well, I'm fighting for my job – I can't just give up, don't want to give up. Anyway I need to go and see him now, try to find what's happening. Wish me luck?'

'You'll be fine, sir. Don't worry.'

Bartlett left to go upstairs. Boase sat staring into space for ten minutes, still toying with the pencil.

After forty-five minutes, Penhaligon knocked on the door and pushed it ajar.

'What is it, Penhaligon?'

'It's Inspector Bartlett – just thought you should know, he's outside sitting down. He came downstairs about ten minutes ago and went straight outside. He don't look too good, I fancy.'

'Thanks, Penhaligon – I'll go out and see him.'

Boase walked out through the front door and saw Bartlett sitting on the wall. He walked over to him.

'What happened, sir? Everything all right – how did it go?'

Bartlett looked away from Boase.

'Sir?'

'I'm finished, Boase.'

'What do you mean ... *finished?*'

240

'I've been told to leave – to take early retirement. All because of what happened with Greet. Apparently his family – should I say, his influential, high-up-in-the-police family – want me gone. If I don't go quietly, they have the power to get rid of me.'

Boase slumped down on the wall next to his boss.

'This can't be right. No, this can't happen – they can't do this to you, sir. After all you've done over the years.'

'They can. They have. I am left with no choice.'

'But I can't believe this, sir. You can't go – you just can't go. What will we all do here – without you?'

'Well, you'll manage, that's what you'll do. They'll bring someone in and it'll be like I've never been here.'

'Please don't say that, sir. There must be something we can do?'

'No. Nothing. Just forget it, Boase.'

Boase stood up and straightened his collar.

'I'm going to see him ... I'm going to see Bolton.'

'Boase – don't be stupid. There's nothing you can do – you'll just irritate him and get on his wrong side.'

'But it's not fair, sir. Anyone can see that. I thought you said this Bolton was a decent sort?'

'Yes, yes I did – but there's nothing he can do. He talked to me for an absolute age about what had happened and what he had tried to do – says he doesn't want to lose me but they're apparently a difficult bunch of people to get along with.'

'Just like Greet then?'

'Just like Greet. Exactly so.'

Bartlett sighed and went on.

'He *tried* to stand in my corner but he doesn't have that kind of power. I'm confident that he's done what he can for me. You'll get on just fine with him, Boase. He's a decent sort – I've got a feeling about him. You know – when you can read someone straight off. I don't think there's any side to him.'

'But I want you to stay, sir. You belong here with all of us.'

'I'm due retirement soon anyway, Boase. You know that – I'm just going a bit early, that's all.'

'But you have another two or three years left, sir, and now you're leaving under a cloud, after all you've given over the years. I'm sorry, it's just doesn't feel right to me.'

'Well, look at it this way – this is an opportunity for me to spend some time with my wife. She needs me and now, well...'

Bartlett cast a look up at Boase. 'Looks like I may still have another woman under my care if you can't sort out this mess with Irene. What do you plan on doing about it?'

'I really don't know, sir. Irene has made it plain she doesn't want me anymore.'

'Well, in that case, all I can say is I'm very sorry. I was very pleased to be welcoming you as a member of my family, I truly was, and so was Caroline. It's such a terrible shame, my boy, a terrible shame.'

By four o'clock the next afternoon, George Bartlett of the Falmouth police force had emptied his desk, said goodbye to all the men who he had come to know so well and taken his hat from the peg for one final time.

By five o'clock that afternoon, Archibald Boase had looked at the diamond engagement he had so recently bought for his girl, kissed it lovingly, and replaced it in the box.

The two men who had carried the Falmouth police so often through frequently troublesome times were now facing their own troubles.

The publishers hope that this book has given you enjoyable reading. Large Print Books are especially designed to be as easy to see and hold as possible. If you wish a complete list of our books please ask at your local library or write directly to:

Magna Large Print Books
Magna House, Long Preston,
Skipton, North Yorkshire.
BD23 4ND

This Large Print Book for the partially sighted, who cannot read normal print, is published under the auspices of

THE ULVERSCROFT FOUNDATION